HONDO COUNTY GUNDOWN

The Valley of the Wolf was no place for strangers, but Chet Beautel was not the usual breed of drifter. He was a straight-shooting man of the mountains searching for something better than what lay behind. Instead, he encountered a new brand of terror enshrouded in a mystery which held a thousand people hostage — until he saddled up to challenge it with a mountain man's grit and courage, backed up by a blazing .45. If Wolf Valley was ever to be peaceful again, Chet Beautel would be that peacemaker.

CHAD HAMMER

HONDO COUNTY GUNDOWN

Complete and Unabridged

LINFORD
Leicester

First published in Great Britain in 2004 by
Robert Hale Limited
London

First Linford Edition
published 2005
by arrangement with
Robert Hale Limited
London

British Library CIP Data

Hammer, Chad
    Hondo County gundown.—Large print ed.—
Linford western library
    1. Western stories
    2. Large type books
    I. Title
    823.9'2 [F]

    ISBN 1–84395–842–2

Published by
F. A. Thorpe (Publishing)
Anstey, Leicestershire
Set by Words & Graphics Ltd.
Anstey, Leicestershire
Printed and bound in Great Britain by
T. J. International Ltd., Padstow, Cornwall

This book is printed on acid-free paper

1

Fangs

Later, it was plain that it was the moose that broke up the Beavertail Trappers' outfit.

If that huge bull had not chosen that moment to appear on the snowy crest above the beaver dam just in time for the first rays of the weak winter sunrise to glint like gold off majestic antlers and bathe its heroic shape in light, Beautel might well have managed to see out his contract.

He wasn't aware of the animal at first. The sun's first rays, which hit this king of the high country like a spotlight, would take several more minutes to drop down to touch the pond, the dam wall and the beaver-trapper.

Chet Beautel stood waist-deep in water so cold he couldn't feel his legs.

The trap stick was floating just beyond his reach some twenty feet below the dam, which concealed a thriving beaver colony. He had tried to hook the damn thing with a stick over long freezing minutes in the half-dark, but in the end had no option but to take the plunge and swim after it.

But the water-level had risen overnight, water was slopping over the dam to create a small current which kept drawing the trap stick into deeper water.

He cursed bitterly.

He was a rangy, long-haired mountain man who loved hunting and far places, hated the cold and was half-way through a planned three-month season trapping for beaver, a season he'd had every grim intention of seeing through until he chanced to glance up to see that damn moose sneering down at him.

The animal looked away with magnificent disdain, the man motionless as he stared up with his strong jaw hanging loose and a sudden leaping sensation in his chest.

He heard himself breathe hoarsely as though someone else was controlling his voice:

'You're a drifter and a loner and you were born just as free as that varmint . . . you ain't a goddamned working stiff!'

This was true. He was a rambling man, descended from generations of ramblers, who had suddenly decided, at twenty-six years of age to rest up his horse, set his hunting rifle aside and take on some steady work for real money like regular folks did.

Because of the moose's arrogance, he might have liked to take out his sixshooter and touch off a couple of shots. But he didn't. He wasn't that sore. In any case, he only ever contracted to go after critters like that if they were busting down somebody's fences or tromping up the farm animals.

But the mere spectacle of the big

critter posing and sneering down at him from its lofty knoll rekindled every footloose instinct, all the wanderlust he'd been stifling for seven murderous weeks up here with Toby, Pete, Clint and Charlie. For the first time in that eternity of frozen fingers, hardtack, buck-toothed chattering beavers and a cold as murderous as a Comanche war party, he suddenly felt like the Beautel he'd always been, knew what he had to do and told the bull moose so.

'I'm all through, you show-off sonuva!' he shouted so loud that icicles dropped from a frozen sycamore. 'I'm goin' drif-tin' again, huntin' mebbe, and just for the hell of it yours might be the first pelt I take!'

He waded out, still shouting and waving his arms for circulation. But the moose continued to soak up the weak sun atop his vantage-point until the sounds of approaching hoofs made him turn disdainfully and disappear with a contemptuous flick of its tail.

Beautel's partners had come hurrying up from the Crooked Creek pond to see what all the hollering was about. They thought he was joking at first about quitting, but ex-trapper Chet Beautel never joked about anything as all-consuming as the inborn wanderlust that had fired the Beautels' boilers, and kept them largely badly paid and on the move through three generations as a consequence.

It was soon all too plain that Charlie, Pete, Clint and Toby would just have to get used to the notion of being without a partner whose skills and energies outstripped those of the four of them put together.

★ ★ ★

It didn't help any that Patterson had stayed too long at the bar at the Chinook saloon before heading home to his shotgun cabin on Wild Horse Ridge. Even sober, Jubilee Basin's most successful wolver and hardened drinker would have had his hands full, the way things turned out. But half-shickered and rollickingly happy as he never was sober, the bearded hill-man was scarcely in any shape to deal with the kind of danger that came stalking through a snowy winter's midnight with a huge moon blazing down while he lay snoring and dreaming about the Chinook's new big, bossy and bad-tempered bar-girl.

The fire was almost out in the fireplace, casting just enough light to pick out the fur rug drawn over the sleeper, the wolf-tails, the enormous buffalo-hide mat before the hearth, the elk-antlers on the walls, the carbine above the door and the old Army issue blankets hanging on the walls, which lent a little color to this masculine hunter's den.

Then with a snort and a sudden twitching motion that brought him up from under his fine fur rug, the hunter was not asleep any more.

Patterson sat stock-still, straining his ears, yet now could not hear anything.

That was what bothered him, shooting little darts of worry into his still-foggy brain as he lowered still-booted feet to the floor. Deep mid-winter nights on the northern slopes of Jubilee Basin, all coldly beautiful now, were never totally silent. So how come it was suddenly as quiet now as if all the normal stirrings of the forest surrounding the lonesome cabin had been shut down, a stillness so unusual that it had penetrated his whiskey-drenched senses and jerked him out of a deep sleep.

He went to the window, taking down his carbine from above the door *en route*. That Hondo County moon he'd ridden home by turned the littered yard bright as day, all cold and still.

Patterson coughed. His temples throbbed and his gaunt and gangly body twitched involuntarily as his mind posed the question: should he go take a look about?

No sooner had his barked 'No!' sent him turning back for his beckoning couch than from the side window he caught a glimpse of something over by the horse barn.

He rubbed the windowpane and peered out.

His eyes strained as he focused on what at first appeared like a patch of shadow against the frosted earth of the yard, only to realize it was not shadow at all but the motionless sprawled shape of his big brown dog.

He grabbed the door-handle and lunged outside.

It was a natural reaction, and he was sobering by the moment as he strode across the yard, avoiding the fur-drying racks where a score of fresh wolf pelts hung, a pile of discarded harness and a long yellow pine box with the words MINNESOTA ANIMAL TRAPS PTY. INC. stencilled in black on one side.

The dog was dead. Patterson glanced swiftly round the yard before making for the barn.

Only then did the last of the whiskey fog leave him, causing him to freeze in his tracks. He turned slowly to stare at the carcass, then back to the cabin, realizing just how far he had come from that solid sanctuary in his haste.

His mouth went dry as a sudden startling suspicion clicked into his brain like a gun hammer cocking — a suspicion that stemmed directly from the reign of terror which had gripped all Jubilee Basin throughout fall and winter, and affected every single man here, even a hardened and bloody-handed hunter like himself.

Had he marched out here voluntarily, or had he been drawn?

He could see through the plank rails of the horse-yard now, saw the dead hens scattered upon the disturbed snow. Dead. His horse was making no sound within the barn. Was it dead also?

He lunged wildly for the cabin with a high choking sound in his throat, then stopped on a dime.

The wolf stood between him and the cabin porch.

'You!'

The way Patterson croaked out the word sounded as though he were addressing another man. It was personal, an acknowledgment of identification passing between two fellow-hunters.

The carbine weighed a ton as Patterson sought to bring it to firing level. He cursed under his breath, ice-cold certain now that Deerkiller, twice the size of a shepherd dog and considered by many to be smarter than any man in the valley, had planned and staged this situation like a general seeking to secure an advantage over an enemy — in this case a successful hunter who killed more wolves every week than any other man in the basin.

A trap! And he had stumbled into it like some blind beast rushing towards the slaughter.

The moon was in the wolf's eyes and Patterson's fingers were as stiff as sticks of jerky. But somehow he touched off the trigger, the gushing flower of orange fire so bright in the cold moonlight, the bullet flying harmlessly over the cabin roof as the wolf rushed and fastened its fangs into his throat.

★ ★ ★

The poster was eye-catching. It read:

KILLER WOLF!
$500 BOUNTY OFFERED
HUNTERS WANTED
THE COUNCIL OF JUBILEE BASIN,
HONDO COUNTY, INVITES ALL
HUNTERS AND TRAPPERS
TO ASSIST OUR CITIZENS HUNT
DOWN THE KILLER WOLF WHICH
HAS ONCE AGAIN TAKEN HUMAN
LIFE. ONLY EXPERIENCED
PROFESSIONALS SHOULD APPLY.
PER ORDER:
MAYOR BUCKNER

'Interested, son?' a voice asked at Beautel's elbow as he stood scanning the poster for a second time.

'Could be. How far to this Hondo County, friend?'

The townsman shook his head.

'You don't really want to know, son.'

'Why not? I'm a hunter and this here advertisement says — '

'No. What it really says, son, plain as the nose on your face, is this: 'Come west to Hondo County and we'll find a coffin to fit you just as easy as we've fitted all the others,' interrupted the man, a hearty fat fellow with spun-silver whiskers and ruddy cheeks. 'That's what it says, no matter how it might read.' His gesture invited the stranger to look around at his tiny, snow-covered township. 'Do you see any civic-minded citizens breaking their necks to ready up and set off west for Hondo here? Or any fool-headed huntsman rushin' to the hardware to buy up all the traps and supplies he can get his hands on — '

'All right, reckon I get your drift. But I'm still askin'. How far?'

The man studied him with keener interest now. He was impressed with what he saw. Six-two of raw-boned mountain man with shoulder-length

12

hair, fringed buckskins and features burnt a deep Rocky Mountain bronze, Beautel had the look of a man of the wilds, hawk-featured with the piercing gaze a man acquired from looking over great distances.

If this was not a genuine huntsman he wouldn't know one if he fell over him, so the towner decided with an appraising nod. And yet he still felt obliged to offer a little more free advice.

'Young feller,' he said urgently, 'I got no doubt that you are the real McCoy. But you gotta know this ain't no everyday appeal those folks out there are makin' and they sure ain't offerin' big *dinero* to the man who can bag any everyday breed of dog wolf, let me tell you.'

'Yeah, I know, pops,' Beautel cut in with a slow smile. 'Let me guess. This critter's a killer and a gorilla and an all-round graveyard-filler — right?'

'Don't joke, boy. This is the real thing. Look, you are a man who knows his wolves, right?'

Know them, partner? he thought, I've hunted them, been hunted by them, trapped, shot, poisoned and even wrassled one or two in my time until I could say I guess I know wolves better than I know most people.

But all he said was, 'Uh huh.'

'Then you'd know that the real wolves, the great wolves of the old forests here in the north country, are mighty intelligent, mebbe the smartest critter on four legs. You agree with that?'

'Guess I have to. That's why I enjoy huntin' them.' He didn't bother explaining that it was less the excitement and danger of the hunt he was interested in so much right now as a reversal of lifestyle that might prove the most important he'd ever make. He'd tried living straight, had made his first serious grab at the things most men his age seemed to hold sacred, and had failed. Now he was switching back to the old footloose way of living he'd followed all his life, and chasing after

14

some 'unkillable' critter sounded just about the right way of getting back to what he'd once been, namely, a man without a star, who nonetheless had always felt like a man, not a goddamn machine.

He arched an eyebrow. 'Why are you still shakin' your head, friend?'

'We're not talkin' any kind of event contest here — take my word for it. This critter who keeps rippin' up cows and horses and hunters — especial wolf-hunters — has been trapped, shot up, poisoned and bad-named so long without it killin' him he's got to be smarter'n God but not half as merciful. Hey, where you goin'?'

Beautel just grinned back over his shoulder as he turned for the saloon nearby, where four familiar figures had just emerged, mountain men like himself.

'Pards lookin' for me, old-timer,' he called back. 'But much obliged for the advice. I'd like to take it only — '

'Only because you're young and you

think you're immortal and you don't know this wolf any better than I know you!' the other responded. 'Well, luck anyways, boy, even though I still reckon you'd be a blamed fool to go after that *dinero.*'

A short time later, this was exactly what Charlie, Clint, Pete and Toby were arguing wearily, even though it seemed a foregone conclusion they weren't going to be able to talk him out of the decision he'd made back in the high country.

The Beavertail Trappers had decided their partner was just overworked and maybe missing some feminine company. So a decision had been made to follow him down to the agency on the prairies, show him a good time, then coax him back up to Serenity and the full six-week stint which would carry them over into the spring.

Faces fell as reality set in, for they needed this man as much for his energy and high spirits as for the fact that they regarded him as the finest camp cook in all Minnesota. But gabby Clint made one last try: was this their rock-solid pard Chet they were talking with now, the golden-bearded young trapper asked rhetorically. Was he genuinely really determined to toss aside the certain rewards of a boom season to go off chasing some murderous old timber-wolf which, according to local hearsay, was a dedicated man-killer who'd proved over and over he simply could not be caught and killed?

He sure as hell was.

So much so in fact that he abruptly decided to pass up the invitation to join them for a farewell session at the saloon, made his hasty goodbyes and went clattering off over the old covered bridge to disappear quickly into the drifts and the blowing snow of a bitter Plains afternoon.

Chet knew he'd been tough, and even if he might not be feeling good about quitting as he pushed the bay along an avenue of mighty, snow-laden elms, at least he was beginning to feel free again — free as that big daddy moose.

They'd made big money from the sale of the fur bales they'd packed down from their winter camp on Serenity Mountain, and stood to double or even treble that return had he chosen to return with four of the best pards a mountain man ever had.

Now he was back on the loose again, mavericking off on a track that sounded like high risk in every way that counted.

Just like it had always been.

He lit up a fragrant stogie, turned his collar up round his ears and passed the lonesome hours casting his thoughts ahead to an unfamiliar place named Hondo County.

He grinned and gusted fog breath into the black sky. Trapping was hard labor, but hunting was more like drifting free with the chance of getting paid for it. And he had to admit this man-killing wolf intrigued him. Deerkiller. He'd never hunted a wild critter with its own name before.

Some time after Beautel quit the cabin compound at Wild Horse Ridge where Patterson the wolf-baiter had been ripped to pieces by Deerkiller, the wind set up a restless moaning through the pine- and cedar-tops.

It was a north-wester blowing out of Canada and it came whistling down over the frozen spines of the ancient Fastness Range. It was an old familiar wind to this north-country man; he could smell it, read it and hear its music as he made his way through the mighty basin feeling like the only spark of life in all this snow-locked emptiness.

Yet the profusion of tracks he followed assured him there was life here in abundance. In truth, it seemed to his keen eye there was more horse- and wolf-sign marking up the snow trails here than he'd ever seen anyplace, particularly that of the wolves, the lobos.

He check-reined the bay to study a

fresher trace line of wolf-tracks angling away between twin beetling knolls. Minute sounds were magnified in the stillness as he tugged his heavy woollen muffler up and over his nose. It was cold country but interesting, this beautiful basin, mighty interesting.

On his way out to Patterson's place he'd encountered a number of hunters, trappers and suchlike camped along the trace of the Pioneer River where it formed the sweeping hook that watered a score or more hardluck-looking spreads and farms. Jubilee Basin plainly bred a rugged brand of citizen, yet most he'd encountered acted like they were intimidated, even running scared of some dumb critter which ran around on four legs and lived in holes in the rocks.

How did you figure?

He soon gave up on the sign-reading and kicked east towards where the great headland of Stagline Bluff appeared against a brooding skyline.

If all these other newcomers, with

their long rifles and a hankering to claim that 500 silver dollars in bounty on its head, were to be believed, then the critter they were hunting was surely sizable. Yet virtually all the tracks he was cutting today were plainly that of young stuff. This was a puzzle he couldn't quite figure as yet. What he was growing sure of, however, was that there were two distinct problems here. Deerkiller was one. The inexplicable explosion in wolf numbers was quite another.

Were they connected? A man would figure they had to be.

According to a local character, Burns Wagons, the man-killer haunted a number of favored hunting ranges, when not occupied in terrorizing settlers, that was. One of these ranges was a belt of dark oak woods five miles south-east of Hardesty, the area he was making for now.

'Deerkiller always hungry,' so the eccentric old Dakota had told him. 'Yet when he kill man he does not consume him. This I understand well. Burns Wagons would never eat white man meat. Yuhk!'

A flicker of a grin touched Beautel's lips at the recollection. Although having spent only a half-day in Hardesty before setting out to get the lie of the land, that had proved long enough for him to absorb some local lore and meet up with several of the more colorful characters of the basin, including the ancient Indian.

According to the storekeeper who'd sold him his provisions, Burns Wagons — who'd apparently earned his name torching prairie schooners along the Oregon Trail decades earlier — had done just about everything to the unlucky West-bound migrants apart from eating them. The storekeeper insisted the Dakota was lucky he hadn't been hanged a dozen times for atrocities attributed to him in the past.

Beautel took all such stories with a grain of salt. He believed only in what he could see, smell, touch, taste — and hunt. He was a practical man of the outdoors. Trailsmen got to be that way. Buffalo dust and fairytales made little impression on someone who dealt with the edgy reality of life every day he lived.

The sound of the shot halted him.

The bay twitched its ears and the rider sat motionless, eyes on a timbered, talus-littered slope at the base of enormous cliffs two miles south-east.

He waited for the sound to be repeated. It wasn't. The landscape lay still and frozen, wrapped in winter silences.

He took out his field glasses and set them to his eyes. Instantly the slope jumped into clearer view and he played his gaze over a massive slab of talus some hundred feet in length by half that distance wide. Trees grew up all around the great slab and something was moving in its shadows.

With deft fingers he worked the adjustment screws. The movement flickered again and Beautel sucked in a sharp breath as the animal sprang into view. It was a wolf, big and black, leaping over a deadfall with its bushy tail rotating the way wolves have when at play or when some piece of sinister lupine mischief is afoot.

Could this be the notorious Deerkiller? So soon? It didn't seem likely. But even an outside possibility was enough for him to touch up the bay with steel and go loping through the snow. He slid his beautiful hunting-rifle from its fringed doeskin scabbard with practised ease.

If these were White Pine Cliffs, as they might well be, then this was yet another alleged killer-wolf haunt, so he'd been told.

What a triumph if he were to flush and bag this critter almost before he'd had time to get to remember where Hardesty's main saloon was situated.

He couldn't help thinking this way. Any hunter who didn't believe himself capable of bagging anything he went after had no business being in the wilds. But as he closed on the tall timber which grew in tiers across the slope, Beautel was not letting enthusiasm run away with him. Every hunter's sense was working overtime as he lifted the bay to clear the gaunt skeleton of a lightning-killed tree before topping out a rise which suddenly brought the full scene into view.

Maybe a quarter-mile distant lay a clearing in close proximity to that monumental talus slab. There was one horse visible where outcroppings of granite thrust aggressively up through the snow, and beyond these another, a riderless dapple-gray, wearing a saddle, which was sliding and threshing its way on its side towards the half-frozen creek at the foot of the slope with three, four . . . five gray wolves attacking it on all sides.

Instantly Beautel looked for the rider. It took but moments to find him. The figure was crouched in a rocky niche some hundred feet above the creek with just one young wolf lurking menacingly close by. Both man and wolf seemed mesmerized by the bloody business taking place below. Beautel knew that when the pack finished with the saddle horse the wolves would concentrate on the man, who seemed to be paralysed by terror.

He was sober as a judge as he jacked a brass shell into the chamber of the rifle before moving in.

He'd thought they might be exaggerating the extent of the wolf trouble in Jubilee Basin, but there could be no denying the predators were here in lethal abundance.

Instinctively he selected the route that would give him the most advantageous position when he drew within range; up by that snow-heavy rocky overhang, then across the hollow and come up atop the bluff well above the creek yet close by the niche.

The rifle was heavy and familiar in his right hand as the nervous bay carried him upwards. They were passing below the looming bulk of the overhang when the horse suddenly skittered sideways downslope, eyes rolling and a scream of pure terror breaking from its throat.

Beautel felt rather than saw the huge shape launch itself from the overhang now looming above him. Trusting instinct, he hurled himself headlong out of the saddle on the downslope side, and the huge wolf's gaping jaws merely grazed his shoulder as it plunged fearsomely close above him in a tremendous dive that saw its great bulk swallowed by a drift as it struck.

The man hit ground hard, rolled, then kicked furiously for the cover of a boulder nearby. His rifle was gone but he managed to rake out his handgun. Pressing his back against the boulder, his hat knocked awry and the muffler covering half his face, he stared about wildly to see the terrified bay struggling to climb the slope, setting up a small avalanche. Through trees and rocks he glimpsed the gray wolfpack now streaming away across the creek below.

No sign of a huge black wolf with a white blaze down its face.

The man up in the niche began bleating like a sick calf.

Beautel was shaking as he rose on one knee. Maybe he'd had closer shaves but could not recall one offhand. But it was less the shock of the near thing that was sending tremors of reaction up and down his spine than his suspicion, maybe more like his certainty, of exactly what had just taken place here.

The juxtaposition of the unhorsed man above and the horse under attack in relation to the overhang where the big wolf had waited on the route Beautel had had to follow upon hearing that shot, made him realize none of it was accidental, no whim of chance.

He sensed this whole attack had been a stratagem employed by the killer wolf to draw him in off the open country in order that it might get to jump him.

But by the time he was upright and recovering his rifle and hat, he was shaking his head. No. Sure, he knew wolves to be amongst the most highly intelligent of all predators, capable of precise tactics and clever strategic planning when on the hunt. But they could not be this smart. That would be giving the lupine species far too much credit, and right now he was in anything but a generous frame of mind.

The one thing he was certain of was that he had come within inches of losing his life.

Welcome to Jubilee Basin!

It took some time to catch his frightened horse, by which time the man, a trapper from Hardesty, had recovered some composure and produced a bottle of rye from his saddle-bags. He had stripped saddle and bridle off the dead horse and was ready to kiss his rescuer's boots.

'Godamighty, stranger, I was a goner fer sure iffen you hadn't come along.' He waved his arms wildly, still agitated despite the soothing effects of a mind-numbing belt of rotgut. 'I was moseyin' in to check me traps in the crik just the way I do every second day, when of a sudden they was all around me, fifteen, mebbe twenty of the varmints all slaverin' and — '

'Not that many.' Beautel was terse. He was having his own reaction to the close call but it was different from the trapper's. He was mad now. He'd been outsmarted by a dumb animal and damn near killed.

'Dozens of 'em,' the fellow babbled on. 'I lost my carbine in the snow and only had three shots in my sidearm and . . . and . . . ' He finally broke off to study his saviour, realizing only belatedly of what a different stamp this stranger was. Long, lean as a whip, buckskinned, long-haired, he appeared calmer in the wake of the incident than any normal man had a right to be.

He snapped his fingers.

'Let me guess. That advertisement they put out after Deerkiller tore up Patterson. You're one of them big-time hunters lookin' to claim his scalp, ain't you?'

'Was that the critter they're after?' Beautel asked, readying the bay.

''Course it was. Ain't they told you the size of him? That was old Deerkiller right enough. And the big bastard sniffed you out on sight, pilgrim. And of course, now I know why them varmints jumped me. They wasn't interested in one beat-up old trapper, no sir. I see it plain as day now. They jest wanted to sucker you in so that hog butcher of a dog wolf could get to run his choppers through your innards before you got to give him no trouble. He does that sort of thing.'

He paused and tapped his temple.

'Thinks perzackly like a man, as you just seen. Like a murderer. Bet you never hunted a varmint with a brain like a man afore, partner.'

No, but I've met men without any brains at all, Beautel said under his breath as he swung up. He was peeved at himself for the way he'd reacted to the incident. He realized now that animals could not reason like human

31

beings, couldn't plan an ambush like a strategist. It was dumb to reckon otherwise. He extended a hand.

'Come on, let's get moving. You can show me the shortest route back to Hardesty.'

The man gabbled all the way back to town but Beautel said barely a word. He was thinking that up until now he'd maybe been taking this challenge a little too lightly. Well, from here on in he was going to be serious. Dead serious, otherwise a man could wind up dead.

2

Mountain Man's Way

'Lone Star steak sauce!' Beautel yelled above the clamor. 'Who ordered the sauce?'

'Ah surely did, Long Hair,' twanged a strong Texan accent, and through the blue haze of cooking fumes, tobacco smoke and the thin smoke rising from the Chinook's big old range appeared the weathered visage of a horse-hunter, gaunt, creased and irascible. Beautel flipped his bottle to the man with one hand while turning over a sizzling steak with the other. The Texan examined the bottle in puzzlement.

'How come a woolly-haired north-country geezer even knows about Lone Star sauce anyways?' he wanted to know. 'And you say you make your own? How can that be?'

Beautel moved from the stove to the cookbench where he was preparing another dish of the trails, son-of-a-gun stew. Impassive faced, Burns Wagons handed him the veal heart and Chet went to work on it with his knife.

'There's men up round Serenity Mountain who won't eat meat without it's soaked in my Lone Star sauce, Texas,' he said. 'And they've never even heard of Texas.'

Everybody laughed, from the fat man behind the bar to the realtor, the cattle-dealer, the party at the round table who called themselves wolf-hunters, as well as two busty Chinook girls who'd been lured from their Sunday morning lie-ins upstairs by the tempting aromas drifting up the saloon's stairwell.

Some Texans had a talent for getting on people's nerves with their incessant bragging, and Hardesty's resident Texan horse-hunter was one of them.

The man glared round, but when he saw his own party chiaking and hooting at him he decided not to make an issue of the implied insult.

'Well, I guess if it's any good in Texas it's gotta travel. Like me.' He unscrewed the cap and tasted the sauce on his finger, eyes popping. 'Man, that's better than I ever tasted. You say you make it yourself, Mister Long Hair? How come?'

Beautel had washed the heart, removed the membrane and excess fat, and was now dexterously cubing it with his big skinning-knife to add to the beef.

'Simple,' he said. He was already growing accustomed to the nickname Burns Wagons had bestowed upon him at first meeting. 'Half a cup of butter, a third-cup of lemon-juice, two table-spoons of black sauce, some garlic, some — '

'OK, OK,' the Texan said, making back for his table, but grinning just the same. 'Gotta tell you they breed 'em strange up here, *amigos*. You'll never get to meet a long-haired young feller what knows how to both cook and hunt at the one time back home in the Lone Star, no siree. Must be somethin' in the water up here.'

'Better hesh up, Tex,' a companion drawled. 'Iffen you get him riled he jest might stop cookin'.'

The Texan accepted the advice, for the only reason this frozen Sabbath in Hardesty had evolved into a boisterous day of good cheer, high spirits and easy camaraderie was the fact that Beautel had shown up looking for breakfast and then revealed himself ready and able to cook it.

The saloonkeeper had taken down the hinged partition separating the saloon's sizable galley from the barroom and with everyone eating and drinking and moving cheerfully from kitchen to barroom, the mood was convivial and relaxed. The cook was enjoying it just as much as anybody.

By this time the sleepy-eyed brunette with the generous measurements had decided he was both cute and interesting, even if he did dress funny.

'So just how did you learn to cook, Mr Beautel?' she wanted to know. 'Wife left you to fend for yourself, I'll wager.'

Beautel was working in rolled-up shirtsleeves, bronzed features glowing from the heat of the range. He took a cigarette from behind his ear and signalled to the old Dakota for a light. Dignified as in everything he did, Burns Wagons soberly lighted a spill of paper and touched it neatly to the weed.

'Mountain men don't wed, sweetheart,' Beautel said, exhaling smoke to add to the companionably fuggy atmosphere.

'Why not? Are they funny?'

'Would be if meet Big Julie,' commented the Chief.

'You know, for a bloody-handed old scalper who used to fry women and children in prairie schooners, don't you think you talk a sight too much, Injun?'

'Should be named Burns Wrong Wagons,' came the poker-faced reply.

Big Julie frowned. 'Why?'

'Me miss wagon that brings Big Julie west.'

This piece of redskin wit was well received, and when the six-feet-two Dakota and the thirty-six, twenty-four, thirty-six bar-girl continued sniping, it diverted attention from the cook, leaving Beautel free to give the wolver his steak then get on with his *pièce de résistance* of the day, the son-of-a-gun stew.

Beautel owed his abilities as a cook, marksman, tracker, trailsman and addicted drifter to his blood-lines.

His father had been one of the first fur trappers to venture into the then hostile mountain wilderness in the early 1800s, and when he produced a son he taught him all he knew about hunting, women, fighting and wandering so successfully that the boy was barely managing to stay out of serious trouble by the time he was twelve years old.

That was the age when inborn wanderlust set the baby-faced Chet drifting and he'd been travelling ever since. He'd been to California, Mexico and New York City by the time he was twenty. He'd sailed on a windjammer round the Horn, fought Indians in New Mexico, run a saloon in Denver and spent two years hunting everything from bear to wolf to buffalo to feed the army and the wagons on the Oregon Trail. Plus half a season trapping — which had been half a year too long.

He looked out.

The snowstorm had struck just on daybreak and now the basin was a world of whirling white.

The stew was almost done when Beautel pricked his ears at the sounds of argument.

The wolvers and horse-hunters were at it again, with the anti-loggers chiming in occasionally from the sidelines.

'Wolvers!' spat a lean-bodied wrangler in fur chaps and a ten-gallon hat. 'Fly-by-night drifters is all you are. We were huntin' the wild horses afore wolves ever got to be a problem here in the basin, and we'll still be makin' a solid livin' at it when you bums and old Deerkiller and the rest of this trouble is gone and forgotten.'

'Just listen to him,' invited a trapper in greasy leathers, turning to his companions. 'Without us keepin' the wolf numbers down there wouldn't be a horse that'd dast come anywhere nigh this basin, and you mama's boys wouldn't be game to go out to the john to take a leak.'

'If you are so all-fired great at your trade,' put in a young fellow dressed like a clerk, 'how is it that even though you've been here most of the winter, just in the past two weeks that devil wolf has killed one man and tried to kill Beautel yonder.'

'Wrong,' a deep voice said in Beautel's ear. 'Not try kill Long Hair. Warn him.'

Beautel stared into the Dakota's sorrel face. 'What?'

'Long Hair new man in basin. Deerkiller give chance. Like he give

Burns Wagons chance once. Wash in river one day, look up and Deerkiller watch from rock this far away.' He stretched long arms wide. 'Look say — try harm me and you die. Tell Long Hair same thing.' The Indian tapped his forehead. 'Spirit wolf. You heed.'

'That's the greatest load of horse crap I've ever heard.'

'I'd listen to old Red Guts if I was you,' an old-timer growled from the corner. 'Take my word . . . all the baitin', shootin' and trappin' is gonna see us git on top of the packs one day, but that killer'll be raidin' still when you boys is old and gray. And for one good reason. He ain't mortal, is what. And you know somethin' else? I got a pow'ful feelin' you sense it already. That right, son?'

Beautel chose to take it all lightly. Grinning around a jawful of fragrant calf-heart and muffled up in a beautiful sheepskin with hatbrim tugged low against the driving snow, he quietly quit the Chinook by a side door and headed along the main street with Burns Wagons.

Yet he'd digested every word. And even though unprepared to listen to any gobbledegook about the man-killer, he did know that critter had stage-managed an ambush for him exactly as a human might. You didn't forget stuff like that.

The town of Hardesty appeared tranquil enough despite its troubles, standing all white and shivery in the wind on a late Sunday morning.

This was a poor community despite the natural richness the basin had to offer. Hardesty was home to a breed of sober, hard-working pioneer folk who liked the way things were and who would rather graft away at earning a living through trade and ranching than sell up to the get-rich-quick industry which had overtaken Ramont Valley to the west.

The lumber trade had consumed the high valley and brought riches for timber tycoon Max Ramont and scarce anybody else. Now Ramont Valley resembled a desert and the timber king wanted to bring his saws, engines and axemen down into the basin, but the valley dwellers said no.

Beautel agreed with them. It would be a crime to strip this fine country even if it was presently polluted by vermin. That thought saw him scratch his neck in puzzlement as he again grappled with a mystery which had been preoccupying this region all year.

How come wolf numbers continued to increase despite the presence of more huntsmen than anyplace in Minnesota?

He grinned as he suddenly realized how seriously he was taking all of this. This wasn't meant to be that way. He'd turned serious and had set out to live like other men just the once, half-way through his twenty-seventh year. Well, he'd reclaimed his freedom, and it sure felt fine as he rode into a town built and maintained by the kind of solid, forward-looking men he knew now he never could be.

A tall building loomed out of the

whirling white. The Hardesty church was a timber and fieldstone construction with a tall bell-tower and a high attendance rate.

Citizens here prayed as enthusiastically as people in other towns drank and, judging by the numbers of parked vehicles outside, the inclement weather had deterred very few today.

Right now they were singing.

Beautel halted. Standing in a world of swirling white with boots wide-planted, he listened as the voices rose and fell and felt a treacherous kick of emotion thinking of the mother he'd never known; the family he didn't have; the normal life he'd finally kissed goodbye to for ever.

'Come, I show you horses.' A guttural voice interrupted his thinking.

The Chief stood with the top buttons of his faded blue tunic, said to have been taken from the corpse of a cavalryman he had slain in some long-ago battle, undone half-way to his waist as though in contempt of the bone-cracking chill.

Beautel knew the Dakota was at odds with most people in the basin for one reason or another, but the old rogue was actually locked in a war with the horse-hunters who rounded up the mustangs of Skyline Plateau and the Cascades for their horse-dealer mayor.

But why this horse-loving, hard-hating former terror of the Oregon Trail had seemingly taken a shine to him, Chet had no idea. Could it be he saw him as a misfit, like himself?

'What horses?' he grunted.

The Chief gestured.

'The mustangs they steal and kill and sell for meat. The same mustangs I rode when I fought the Bluecoats. They my brothers. But for mustangs Chief would now be gone.'

'You mean, back to the tribes?'

'To the ages!' Burns Wagons intoned dramatically, raising long arms to stormy skies. Then he slumped again. 'Long Hair come see. Maybe we set free today.'

Beautel backed up a step.

'You're cracked. Why would I do somethin' crazy like that?' Without waiting for a response, he swung towards the church. 'In any case, I'm goin' in here. You can come too if you know how to behave.'

But the Dakota only sneered.

'Maybe Chief wrong about Long Hair. He think you warrior but now you talk like squaw.'

'You weren't as mouthy when you were wolfin' down my son-of-a-gun stew.'

The red face showed contempt. 'Long Hair cooks. Does he think that make him a man?' Then he relented, almost smiled. 'Good stew though.' He raised a hand. 'Hau!' he grunted and was gone in the whiteness, leaving Beautel shaking his head and heading for the church.

The fierce gust of wind that boosted him through the doors blew snow half-way along the aisle. Every head turned as he fought to shut the doors behind him, but to their credit, their singing didn't falter.

It was 'Rock of Ages' and they were giving it all they had, easily drowning out the storm sounds with wheezing organ and lusty voices. The churchgoers of the basin dressed for the occasion, men in boiled shirts and velvet-collared jackets, the womenfolk in their Sunday best with shiny-faced children about them, all angelic-looking in the candle-light but doubtless as bloody-minded and devious as were children all over.

The one item of male apparel not in evidence until the arrival of the most recent wolf-hunter to respond to the council's appeal, was the hat.

Preacher, acolytes and worshippers were to a man uncovered, a fact which Beautel was unaware of until a severely attractive woman standing in a nearby pew with a half-sized boy turned her head and hissed:

'Uncover in the Lord's house, sir!'

That was his first meeting with Mrs Lydia Creighton, a farming lady whose husband had disappeared some years earlier. The woman attended church regularly always with her young son Louis and sometimes, as was the case today, she was accompanied by the lumber king of Hondo County, Max Ramont.

The drifter got to know these things when the preacher sought him out at the end of the service to enquire anxiously if he'd had any success with the killer wolf.

Accompanying the reverend was the tall bespectacled gentleman who'd interrogated Beautel closely about his qualifications and plans upon his arrival.

Nathan Pooley was editor of the *Basin Herald* and a man dedicated to the well-being of the community and its battle against the wolf plague.

It was while he was speaking with Pooley in the vestibule that the woman, boy and the expensively dressed lumber king came by, and the newsman insisted on making introductions.

The kid couldn't stop smiling; he

thought Beautel looked like a hero from his storybooks with his height, long hair and buckskin jacket.

Lydia Creighton was cool and aloof. Could be she was reflecting on just what strange types the basin's problems were attracting these days.

Ramont proved neither effusive nor aloof. His handshake was strong but without warmth and he lost no time in warning Beautel that the wolf problem was insoluble. Claimed the wolves would continue killing stock and people and scaring away newcomers in their hundreds until it would be a case of 'last one out turns out the lamps.'

'Umm,' Beautel murmured, when Lydia Creighton spoke up.

'Please, we're all too well aware of your pessimistic views on our problems, Maxwell. In any event, according to what I read in your paper, Nathan, Mr Beautel seems convinced he will per- sonally solve all our concerns before the spring. Is that not so, Mr Beautel?'

Beautel smiled at her.

'Seems I made that statement before I visited White Pine Cliffs, ma'am. Since then, I've been learnin' to keep my eyes wider and my mouth shutter.'

'Mom,' said the kid, 'is shutter a word?'

'Hush, son.'

Then Louis Creighton said eagerly, 'Is it true what they are saying, mister? Did Deerkiller really get to knock your hat right off your head?'

'That's what I was about to ask, Chet.' The newsman smiled. 'Great story if it's true.'

Beautel made a rueful face at the boy. 'Sorry to admit it, but it's true, kid. There I was, lopin' along watchin' this trapper, and next thing I know somethin' half the size of a bear is swoopin' right over me like the biggest bird a man ever saw — '

'Then by your own admission, you had your opportunity and let it slip?' the woman enquired.

Beautel's jaw went slack. 'Er, yeah, I guess you could put it that way, ma'am.'

'I said it at the time, Mr Pooley, and I'll say it again,' Lydia said stiffly, 'that huge bounty posted by the council is worse than useless. All it has succeeded in doing is to attract all sorts of anti-social types to our town to drink and wassail while our problems multiply out of hand.'

'Wassail?' Beautel frowned. 'What's a wassail?'

'You're quite right, Lydia,' Ramont interrupted. 'If your wolf problem was solvable it would have been overcome long ago.' The man glanced sharply at Pooley. 'I hate to say I told you so, Mr Pooley, but surely it's plainer than ever by now that lumber is the only way for the basin to go.'

'Over my dead body,' retorted the newsman.

'And mine also, Maxwell,' the woman said reprovingly. At that point a snow gust hit the church wall and she reached down to pat her son's curly head. 'It's time we left. I hate to be away from the place too long these days.' She gave Beautel a final disapproving look. 'For obvious reasons. Good day, gentlemen. Come, Louis.'

'But I want to see his guns, Mom.'

'Come along, I said!'

'Another time, kid.' Beautel grinned. Then he heard himself boast: 'And don't you folks fret none, that wolf won't bother you much longer.'

'Hold up, Lydia, I'll walk you to your rig,' Ramont called. He nodded brusquely to Beautel. 'I'd be ready to wager you'll be proved wrong on that one, mister. Your breed have been coming and going all winter yet today there are more wolves about than ever.'

'And you seem real cut up about that, Ramont,' was Beautel's edgy response.

'I just want what's best for most people,' the lumberman said, walking away. 'I'm yet to encounter one of your breed who thinks that way.'

'Well, I handled that pretty well, Nathan,' Beautel said wryly as the party quit the vestibule in a flurry of snowflakes. 'Riled her and got ticked off by him, while the kid reckons I'm a bit of a failure. Guess I'll have to do better if I want to see a statue of myself go up in the main street here one day, huh?'

The newsman laughed.

'I reckon that we could both use a stiff one, Chet,' he suggested. 'And while we're at it I might pick your brains about wolves and their habits.'

'Sounds good to me,' said Beautel, fitting his hat to his head as they made for the church doors. 'What do you want to know?'

'Mainly how hunters and trappers can account for up to a dozen wolves here in any given week while they're chasing Deerkiller, yet all this culling only seems to increase their numbers.'

Nothing original about the man's concern, Beautel reflected. He'd been pondering the mystery ever since his arrival. Too bad he still didn't have even the hint of an answer. Maybe they'd only understand it all after he'd bagged this five-hundred-dollar wolf which seemed to think just like a man.

3

Wolf Hate, Wolf Death

The bearded trapper slogged through the drifts that piled deep in the long, blue-tinged shadows of the bluff. The day was crippling cold and the man's breath rasped in his throat as he plodded along, head down, snowshoes leaving huge dinosaur prints in the crusted snow.

This high track offered a matchless view of the basin all the way along the river to the rearing escarpment of Skyline Plateau. But the trapper wasn't interested in scenery, just the $500 bounty he was chasing along with the fame success would bring, which in turn he hoped would assist him break down the resistance of that handsome big blonde at the Chinook, the one who treated him and all his unwashed kind like social lepers.

A half-mile south, where the man had carefully laid his trap, the silver wolf sat quietly, waiting to die. It was a female with bright yellow eyes and young, as were most of the Jubilee Basin wolves.

Yet even at just a little over a year in age, the animal possessed all the innate wolf wisdom which characterized the species, which was why it merely sat there waiting for death instead of foolishly fighting the trap which held its foreleg with its cruel steel jaws.

The wolf had had but a brief journey yet was mature enough to know both hate and love; hate of man and love of all else; the snow, the green summer mornings, the swift rush of the hunt, the companionship of the packs.

Now it was over and it sat impassive and full of hate, waiting to see the man who had brought it to the end of its brief, wonderful journey, ready to hate the man with total ferocity until the very moment of death.

The man appeared, yipped with excitement then slumped with bitter disappointment.

For just one five-hundred-dollar moment the trapper thought he'd caught the man-killer, but a second glance showed it was merely a very large and handsome young wolf.

'Just a bitch!' he muttered, drawing his revolver.

He did this with his left hand even though he was by nature right-handed. But the right hand, hidden inside a fur mitten, was missing three fingers and half a thumb as a result of one occasion when he had tried to take a live wolf from a trap and was savaged for his pains.

The wolf did not rise but simply sat there with the ice wind stirring its silver ruff — staring relentlessly as the trapper cocked his weapon.

Meeting the unblinking yellow gaze the man could feel the animal's implacable hatred, and this caused his gun hand to shake a little.

All this for twenty dollars, he thought bitterly as he steadied the gun. So much brutal work and relentless cold just to bag a single week's provisions money. There might have been some pleasure in the moment if the trapped animal were to whine, snarl or attempt to chew its forefoot off, but the way it stared at him in its last moments made him feel that the critter was the winner and he somehow the loser.

'Where's the big bastard?' he suddenly shouted. 'Your last chance, wolf. 'Fess up where he's hidin' out and I'll set you free. Where is Deerkiller, you motheaten floor rug?'

The wolf just stared until the gun spewed flame and its journey was at an end. As the sound of the single shot reverberated from one cliff to another and coveys of winter birds flew high with cries of alarm, the trapper stared off along the basin to see in the far distance the small black dots of movement working their way along the north side of the Pioneer River.

More wolves.

His shoulders slumped and he shook his head. There was something downright creepy about all this. No matter how many a man killed there were always more. How did they do it? He shook his head and shivered inside his buffalo robe. It might well be that, unable to make more than grubstake here, and with the big brassy blonde ignoring all his overtures, he would have to think seriously of hauling his freight and moving on.

Many other hunters had already come and gone, he knew. He'd met some of the quitters. All spoke of the same things — the seeming immortality of the killer wolf, the wolf numbers, the constant sensation of being watched no matter where they travelled in the basin — a feeling he had right now.

It was eerie and unnatural and by the time he'd taken the bounty scalp and was heading back for his horse and sled, he'd definitely made up his mind to quit.

* * *

Where a slab of stone thrust out from the basin wall high above the river, the killer wolf sat watching its world in the morning.

It had seen the man, heard the shot and knew another sister was gone. Already these small things were locked away in the reservoir of wolf memory and would remain untouched until perhaps some fresh encounter should demand that the remembrance be drawn upon to fan his rage.

What it had seen that morning was unremarkable and oft-repeated. They came, they killed, they tried to kill him and they failed. It was the rhythm of the valley, something as familiar as his own slow pulse-beat.

A small growl escaped the deep chest as piercing eyes focused on the scene across the river. A deer was on the run with a trio of graceful young wolves in pursuit. But the deer was swift and terrified and was gradually drawing away as its flight carried it towards a clump of thick bracken.

Deerkiller's blue eyes blinked. Even his wonderful wolf vision could not detect the danger lurking in the bracken, yet knew it had to be there. For this was how hunting wolves worked; if they could not run prey down they resorted to tactics. Suddenly two lethal shapes erupted from the bracken so explosively that the foolish, frightened deer could only leap high in terror, and when it came down it fell into their jaws.

Soon the deer was just a red smudge on the snow and the pack was moving off south, relaxed and happy with full bellies.

And Deerkiller growled again.

This was all his range, twenty miles one way by ten the other. His dominant kind naturally took command of a space as large as they needed to support their hunting, and their normal custom was to hunt in a big circle in order not to deplete the game at any one point beyond its ability to recover.

Back in the wolf's memory was the time when it had been this way in the basin, and it would drive off or swiftly kill any other wolf which threatened its preserves.

Not any more.

Now he regarded the wolf packs as his allies in the eternal war of attrition against the common enemy. They were terrified of him yet he let them run riot where they might.

It now knew where they sprang from, as he knew so many things. Such as where man was most likely to set his traps, where he hunted; his strengths, foolishnesses, habits both everyday and strange. This intimate knowledge and understanding of the enemy rendered him almost invincible. Yet the great wolf knew he would never be that. For this intelligence which transcended that of other wolves told him that there were men, who stood above other men, as he stood above lesser animals.

One particular man-thing of this kind

had come to the basin recently and Deerkiller had had his chance to kill him at the outset. Instead, undermined by some strange empathy for a solitary creature which seemed so much like itself in some inexplicable way, the big wolf had chosen not to kill but instead issue a warning.

The fact that the warning had failed, and that for weeks now this tall man-thing had been solitarily riding on his spoor, visiting his secret places, appearing and disappearing with a skill matching his own — made him again aware of his own vulnerability which he shared with all living things.

Including man.

Or in this case, in this cruel winter-time, one man.

For reasons it would never understand, it had not wanted to kill this man-thing with the yellow hair which seemed somehow like itself. Now he knew he must kill, and do it soon in order that Deerkiller would feel supreme again, king of the basin and lord of the lesser wolves once more.

Effortlessly he rose from his rock slab and vanished into the winter trees as swiftly and silently as smoke.

★ ★ ★

Sitting his horse at the edge of a rhododendron thicket on the north rim of the range which separated basin and valley, Chet Beautel was momentarily stunned by the ugliness he was seeing.

He'd quit Jubilee Basin, winter-locked yet rich and verdant beneath the snow, covered a mile-high climb to cross the rearing Skyline Plateau to reach the high valley beyond which, once beautiful, was now a scene of utter desolation, a new and grotesque land-scape hacked out of the Minnesota landscape by saw and axe.

Ramont Valley. It had once been known as Blackfoot Valley before lumber boomed and a man who knew about lumber took over here.

In certain quarters, particularly down-stream at booming Milltown, which was growing rich on the timber trade, Ramont was a hero of the new time, a prince of commerce and hope of the future. Or least-ways it seemed that way to Beautel, who was growing more familiar with the region every day. By now he figured he knew almost everything except how to bag a certain he-wolf, he mused with a wry grin.

Three weeks of ceaseless riding had furnished him with an intimate knowledge of the killer's far-reaching range, its habits, hideouts, manifest strengths and supposed weaknesses — yet not one single glimpse of the critter to brag about.

Yet all that time he'd been living with the sensation, intuition — call it what he might — that Deerkiller was watching him, maybe stalking him at times, certainly plotting his eventual destruction.

He'd needed a diversion from failure, so had turned his back on the basin and made his way up to the logging country here in the shadow of Fortress Mountain.

During his long climb from Hardesty, Beautel had sighted perhaps a dozen wolf packs, some hunting, others resting, several merely loitering in the snowy woods.

Up here, of course, there wasn't a wolf to be sighted. Nothing for them here. Nothing for anybody now, by the looks.

He stiffened on sighting the riders. There were three of them and they were climbing rapidly towards his slope where he sat the bay in clear view by the thicket.

He sat easy in the saddle, narrow-eyed and frowning. Simply the way the men rode and the expressions on tough faces warned him this was no welcoming committee.

He glanced behind and upwards. Plenty of time to get gone. But why run? He was up here looking for something, wasn't he? He might not be sure just what it was, but you didn't get to find out much by high-tailing, that was for sure.

The horsemen reached his level and approached at a jingling trot. One sported a garishly checked woollen jacket but the other two were in weathered mackinaws and flat-brimmed hats, hard-bitten fellows all three. Security, was his guess.

'Who the tarnal are you?'

No friendliness here. Suspicion and aggression. He could handle that. Wrestling with scalp-hunting Blackfeet or finding a thousand-pound bear peering through your tent flap on a chill spring morning taught a man not to scare easy.

'Beautel. I'm from the basin.'

'Told you it was him,' one mackinaw said to the other. 'We'd best take him down to see the boss.'

'Reckon Max'd want to see him?'

'I know he said he didn't like the cut of this joker's jib after meetin' him in town.'

They were discussing him as though he wasn't there. Beautel was starting to peeve.

'Ramont said that, did he?' he asked. 'That's disappointin', on account he struck me as a real gent. You know, the help the poor, tend the sick kind of pilgrim. I thought I impressed him.'

Three pairs of eyes surveyed him bleakly. Was he some kind of smartacre, or what?

Beautel traded stare for stare. Plainly the husky fellow in the plaid jacket was in charge, a mustachioed hard man of his own age sporting unmatched weapons. The right-hand one was a Remington .44 with the trigger guard cut away, for close-range work. The left one was a Peacemaker '73 with a seven-inch barrel that he carried backward and cross-pulled with his right hand for long-range work in lieu of a saddle rifle.

Not just security, badasses, so he decided. But why would a timberman want men of this stamp on his payroll?

Then he remembered. Newsman Nathan Pooley and others hinted that Ramont had a rep for enforcing business deals with strongarm methods. That he'd had big trouble with the Milltown law on more than one occasion. They warned that the timberman should be treated with considerable respect. Face to face with this trio, Beautel reckoned he could understand why.

Finally Plaid Shirt reached a decision.

'Let's go,' he grunted, shifting his horse to provide Chet room to precede them off the ridge. 'Come on, mountain man, we don't have all day.'

He could have resisted but didn't. He wasn't sure why Ramont and his valley interested him, but they did. The man wanted the timber rights to the basin, yet they wanted no truck with him down there. Seemed to him that a man like this wouldn't just stand back and accept refusal without putting up a fight.

But maybe he was wasting time, he reflected as he led the way down.

Hunting was his business here, not lumber. And he did not need reminding that his business was not doing all that well.

The trail led them across to the river.

Ahead Beautel saw that a ranch house of whip-sawed lumber had been added to and changed to become an office and living-quarters for the company's buckers and fallers. A cavvy of saddle mounts shared spacious yards out back of the building, along with heavy percherons used for snaking sawlogs out of the woods.

This was a big operation, would have had to be to fell and shift so much lumber.

A man-made lake formed a holding pond for the cut logs, although it was largely empty at this part of the season.

From across the river and high up the largely denuded slopes, he could hear the steady ring of twobitted axes as Ramont's crews cleaned up what was left of the commercial lumber. The sudden cry of 'Timber!' came running down the breeze, followed by the shuddering crash of a ponderosa pine striking the earth with great force.

The hazing smoke from idling donkey engines drifted across the headquarters compound ahead; squat, ugly engines which nevertheless were capable of snaking enormous logs into the creek for floating to the holding dam. The surface of the wide and shallow pond reflected the snow slopes where men in the traditional lumberjack's working rig of woollen plaid shirts, big caulked boots and knit caps moved about sluggishly.

With a perceptive eye, Beautel saw that Ramont's operation here was rapidly winding down, its impressive facilities largely underemployed.

'Yonder's the boss,' he heard one of the mackinaws say behind him. Then, 'Hey, Long Hair, you show Mr Ramont some respect now, hear?'

He didn't respond. Yet it didn't pass his notice that they seemed aware of the nickname Burns Wagons had given him, and which the town had picked up. He was puzzled. Why should just another wolver in the basin seem important enough for these lumber heavies to know this much about him, sight unseen?

Ramont stood on the gallery of the made-over office, well-dressed, smoking, the long-boned face somber as he watched the party come in.

Around his tall figure were gathered several unshaven cousin jacks, honing axes, toying with an engine part, one huge Scandinavian with a shock of corn-colored hair doing a pretty second-rate job of shoeing a mule.

No doubt about it. For an outfit which the *Basin Herald* had recently described as 'Like a gigantic funnel, tapping the thousands of acres of once pristine timberland up in the valley, denuding the land of its sheltering trees in such a ruthless and large-scale manner as to ensure that erosion and drought would surely follow spelling the ruin of the land for future generations for all time . . . ' Ramont

Lumber was definitely staggering along in low gear.

'Get down, trapper,' ordered one of his escort as they swung down before the compound. Beautel remained in the saddle. A mackinaw made towards him but the other called him back. The three stood to one side as Ramont quit the gallery and crossed to them, hands resting on his hips as he stared up at Beautel.

'We meet again, drifter.'

'Looks like.' Beautel hooked a leg over his pommel and took out his durham. 'Why the reception committee, Ramont? You figure I might steal a tree or somethin'?'

'Mr Beautel has a rustic sense of humor, boys,' Ramont declared. 'Which of course in itself is harmless. Yet I'm not sure you are harmless, mister. I mean, you're quite sure you were brought in as a wolf-hunter, are you? You wouldn't be something else, by any chance?'

Chet frowned. Something else? What

might that be? He chose to skirt around the query.

'Guess most of us wear more than one hat at times. You for instance, Ramont.'

'That is Mr Ramont to the likes of you, drifter,' interjected Plaid Jacket.

'It's all right, Darcy,' Ramont said smoothly. 'We have to make allowances for wild men from the hills.' He paused and shot Beautel a suddenly sharper look. 'What are you doing up here? Spying?'

Beautel torched his hand-rolled into life and squinted an eye.

'What's eatin' on your liver?' he retorted. 'A man moseys in all quiet and peaceful, scarce has time to see what a god-awful mess you jokers have made of this place, next thing I'm saddled with a reception party that drags me down here so you can sound off at me. Back in the mountains, we'd count that sort of welcome downright unfriendly.'

'Keep away from Mrs Creighton, bum.'

Beautel almost dropped his smoke. 'Huh?'

'I saw you eying her off and playing up to the kid. That sort of thing doesn't wash with me. And if you are just a wolf-hunter, and not some weird brand of protection the basin has imported, stick to your knitting and stay to hell and gone away from my valley. And finally, Mr Long Hair, if I hear one whisper of you taking sides in the debate on whether the basin will or will not sell me their timber leases, you'll wish you'd stayed in the mountains. Do I make myself clear?'

Beautel was intrigued. The timberman was hinting at matters he had little knowledge of and certainly no involvement in here.

He took another leisurely glance around. By this time his audience had swelled to around twenty. But apart from his welcoming committee, the others appeared pretty much as he expected timber workers to be: husky, interested enough but basically straight

— if he were any judge.

But Max Ramont was something else. He had no doubt now that he was a genuinely ruthless man accustomed to getting what he wanted. He didn't want to tangle with him, had no intention of doing so. But he knew he would not be forgetting this meeting. And he would not be told what he could or could not do, either.

'Reckon I'll be moseying,' he said quietly.

'What if I said no?' countered Ramont.

'Look, Ramont, I'm an easy-goin' guy but you are startin' to get up my — '

'All right,' Ramont cut in, turning for the office. 'I'll see you around, hunter. But don't forget what I said. Darcy, see the man off.'

'I'll find my way out,' Beautel said, kneeing his horse through the ring of bystanders. 'I'm a tracker by trade, remember?'

'I'm seein' you off, Long Hair.'

He checked the bay as Darcy drew abreast and reined in. Beautel the easy-going wolf-hunter was fading and the mountain man in him was rising.

He spoke softly but with force.

'Get out of my daylight, horse's ass. I've had about all I can swallow of you cousin jacks for one day.'

Darcy flushed hotly and swung a punch. Before the blow could reach its target, Beautel whipped up a big, high-heeled riding-boot lightning-fast and rammed it into his guts. Hard.

As Darcy crashed to ground Beautel heeled the bay away and was well clear of the headquarters before Ramont's man could struggle back on his feet, his face the color of old pipeclay.

Beautel struck north-east. Nobody followed as he loped along the slushy trail, which was not to say he was home free. Anything but. The bizarre-looking character seated in a wired-over dogcart had witnessed the entire incident below, and consequently had grabbed up a carbine from the rig's rifle-clasp.

The weapon was trained squarely on Beautel's chest as he entered the trees. Reluctantly he drew up; his pressure gauge rose another dangerous notch.

'What?' he demanded. He was wary, for this man looked dangerous, a vast unshaven pilgrim in greasy leathers and matted black buffalo coat with a nose like a melon. The hairy hands clutching the carbine were the size of wombats.

The apparition didn't reply. Instead he stood in the cart to bring the compound in sight and pumped a shot into the sky.

'It's all right, Whiskey!' the distant voice of Darcy hollered. 'You can leave the bastard pass!'

'Whiskey?' queried Beautel as the carbine came down. His eyes ran over the bloated figure, and he couldn't help sniffing. 'That your handle?'

'Tom Whiskey is the name and lumber is my game.'

'You don't look like lumber to me.'

One eye shut tight and its companion popped and rolled.

'And what might I look like to you, mountain man?'

But Beautel had suddenly seen enough of this valley and its denizens for one day.

'You look almost like a mountain man yourself!' he called back as he heeled away. 'Except we bathe twice a year whether we need it or not.'

'And foul cess to you, Long Hair!'

Another who knew his nickname. Again Beautel was puzzled. Yet as the long-legged bay climbed up through the forest of gray stumps, some of them monsters up to twenty feet across, he felt something else command his thoughts and he kept sniffing, recollecting the stink of the gross man which would turn the stomach of a hog. And now he was concentrating, the answer came lightning-fast.

This brought a puzzled frown as, with the valley behind now, he reined in and slid to ground to rest his mount following the steep climb.

He'd been told there had been no

wolves up here in the high valley since Ramont hauled in his first donkey engine, yet the fellow named Whiskey, who plainly belonged there, had smelt more like a wolf than a man.

4

Daggers Drawn

Late afternoon.

Beautel travelled in a wide circle across the basin, veering away from Hardesty all the while without actually admitting to himself where he was heading.

A mile back he'd stopped off to examine an abandoned ranch house with snow piled high all around and groaningly heavy on neglected roofs.

It was the third such he'd sighted during his return from Ramont Valley, each desolate scene telling its own story. At the second place abandoned, a sad notice nailed to the front door revealed why the ranchers had gone: *On account of poor prices, high taxes and wolves, wolves, wolves.* He'd actually disturbed a pack of five youngish wolves slinking about on some sinister lupine business of their own, fleeing when they saw him coming, then taunting him with their voices from the hills when they were safe.

The contrast between valley and basin could scarcely have been sharper. The former ugly and prosperous, the latter shimmeringly beautiful as only highland Minnesota could be, yet here, good, poor folks were forced to walk off their land.

He crested a snow-smooth slope to see natural drama unfolding directly below: a laboring buck with two gray wolves closing in for the kill.

Chet swung his rifle to his shoulder. He was a crack shot. The closer wolf died in one convulsive leap which left a twenty foot crimson smear on the virgin snow. As its companion rushed frantically away from the echoing snarl of the shot, Beautel triggered twice more, and the handsome buck was his.

Only then did he finally admit to himself the reason he'd taken the long way home to Hardesty. The strange reason which he expected to regret.

★ ★ ★

'Wolves?' Lydia Creighton had a precise inflection in her voice as she watched her unexpected visitor quarter the skinned, gutted and river-washed deer he'd brought in from the old Mulligan place. 'You say this man smelt of wolves?'

'Keerect. Hey, kid, pass me that bowl, will you?'

'His name is Louis, Mr Beautel.'

'Sure it is.' Chet winked at the kid who was following his every stroke with the knife and smiling with delight. It was not every day someone arrived here with a fresh carcass over his shoulder, dressed like a storybook hero. The child's wide eyes focused on the four-inch wide leathern belt with a holstered revolver hanging on one side and a sheath for a ten-inch Shoshone skinning-knife on the other.

Beautel accepted the bowl, gave another wink and went on cutting.

'So, what do you make of that, ma'am?' he persisted. 'Any notion who that Whiskey feller might be?'

Lydia Creighton had had a hard day. Every day was hard for a lone woman trying to run a ranch, raise a son and keep her head above water in a region where folks on the land were going to the wall every month.

She would not admit it, of course, but she was all but drooling at the sight of thick venison steaks being piled one atop the other as that wicked Indian knife performed its work so slickly one almost expected it to stand up and whistle Annie Laurie as an encore.

But of course there was no such thing as a free lunch. Or in this case, a free supper. Plainly Mr Long Hair Beautel expected to be invited to break bread with the family after providing the wherewithal for the meal — and perhaps for as many as twenty future meals for mother and son.

How dare he presume so.

Yet as she sighed and unfolded her arms, Lydia knew she was vastly more pleased than displeased by this unexpected turn of events. She turned to go inside and ready the greens, belatedly realizing that Beautel was looking up at her from the work bench with eyes the color of blued steel.

She realized he was waiting for an answer.

'Look, Mr Beautel — '

'Chet. You call me Chet and I'll call you Lydia. Nice name, that. I'll wager you know that Whiskey fellow, Lydia.'

'Only by sight, fortunately.' Lydia Creighton sniffed disapprovingly.

'Mom and I saw him one day in Hardesty, Chet,' the boy piped up.

'The name is Mr Beautel, Louis,' she reproved.

'Chet will do fine,' he said.

'The fellow was drunk and offensive, naturally,' the woman supplied. 'Harassing women on the streets, starting fights, the usual sort of things that men of that calibre get up to in a strange town.'

Beautel paused in his work. Was she hinting he was that type? Maybe he was being too sensitive? Since meeting this stern, strong woman in Hardesty he had been aware of just how different she was from the general run of female he'd congressed with over the hunting seasons, coming down out of the Rockies with a huge bundle of pelts and lusts, hungers and raging thirsts clamoring for satiety.

'What happened?' he wanted to know. 'Someone buffalo him, I guess?'

'There was nobody capable of doing that unfortunately. As you know, we don't have a sheriff in Hardesty. We rely on the sheriff of Milltown and his deputies to maintain law and order here, and by luck Sheriff Henley arrived late that afternoon on other business.' Lydia smiled pleasurably at the recollection. 'He took to Tom Whiskey with his gunbarrel, then kicked him out of town, literally, warning him to never come back. And he has not been back, I'm happy to say.'

'Hmm,' murmured Beautel, wrinkling his brow. He slipped his wicked Shoshone knife away. 'You don't happen to recall that feller smellin' of wolf that day, do you?'

'Really, Mr Beautel, would you expect a person to notice something like that? Is the meat ready?'

It was.

Beautel toted it inside and Lydia immediately set about preparing the meal. He had not been invited to join them, but neither had he been invited to leave. So he stayed on. He'd stopped by on impulse, stayed on for the same flimsy reason. Sure, he'd thought about these people he'd met at the Hardesty church and was concerned to know how a woman and child alone might be faring, especially as the wolf problem appeared to be worsening by the day.

But concern was not the only thing that drew him here, he was honest enough to admit as he sauntered outside to see what the kid was doing. The day before he'd been fraternizing with a bad old Dakota whose life was just as odd and unnatural as a mountain man's, today had been spent at Ramont Valley amongst hardcases who were anything but regular Westerners.

A need for normalcy was the reason he'd come calling on the Creightons, or so he chose to believe.

It was a simple place out here on the little creek — house, barn, stables and yards.

But by no stretch of the imagination, he must admit, could it be said to look normal.

The windows were covered in heavy wire mesh, and rusted bob wire was strung along the top of the rickety fence surrounding the headquarters. Gun ports were cut in the walls, and he'd glimpsed no fewer than three rifles, two .32s and an ancient smoothbore trade gun inside.

There was one horse, which they

locked in the sturdy barn at night, and lying within sight of the back porch on a slope, protruding from the snow, were the skeletal remains of a steer slain by the wolves.

Even so, the little spread was typical of many Beautel had seen across the basin, those which had not yet been abandoned, that was.

In some ways Jubilee resembled a war zone where the enemy was close by: the emphasis was on security and defence — and living here for people like this must be a bloody nightmare.

So, what made them stay?

He grinned at that thought as he rolled a cigarette on the back porch. He knew the answer well enough. It was called the pioneering spirit. It was strong enough to smell in the very air down here. These might be ordinary, everyday people but they had grit in their gizzards. They'd done battle with blizzard, drought, failed crops, cattle disease and, in the past, redskins. These days it was a wolf plague apparently led by a giant rogue of a Western timber wolf which some of the more jittery pioneers were beginning to invest with supernatural qualities.

But still they stayed and Beautel liked that. It was called surviving. Kids left motherless and eventually fatherless before they were half-grown learned to survive early and so learned to admire it in others.

It was coming on dark. Beautel took the boy on a patrol of the headquarters, checking out the fences, putting the bay and the ranch horse away, collected eggs from the chicken run.

Louis talked non-stop. He wanted to know all about beaver trapping, wolving, buffalo hunting and scalp-taking Indians with headdresses reaching down to their hips and howls to turn any man's blood to ice.

Chet obliged the child with some solid facts mixed in with a few outrageous lies, and Louis was rosy-cheeked and laughing when they were finally called into supper. They didn't talk that much, yet the atmosphere in the small neat room with the fire blazing in the hearth and A-grade venison doing its soothing work, was easy and comfortable.

An hour passed, and Lydia was stacking the dishes when the boy nodded off at the table. She took him inside to bed and Beautel rose from his chair and flicked his cigarette butt into the fire. Time to go, mountain man; don't overstay your welcome.

The framed daguerreotype on the mantel showed the woman and boy standing outside with a tall man in a dark coat. He'd been told in town that the husband and father had gone gold-hunting in Canada and was missing, believed dead.

He was flicking his long hair back and sitting his Stetson on the back of his head when the woman returned.

'Oh,' she said politely. 'Going?'

'Yeah. And much obliged.'

'Thank you for the meat. We haven't had venison in . . . well, never mind that. You will ride carefully, won't you. It is dangerous at night, even for a mountain man.'

He searched for hint of irony or disapproval in her tone, didn't find any. He knew she found him an odd one, the way he dressed and the hair. But tonight these did not seem to bother her too much. Or maybe she was just relaxed to have a man about the place for a change.

She was showing him out to the porch when it happened, the sort of sound that once heard was never forgotten.

It began as a long quavering cadence of total melancholy, a mournful feral howl which came tumbling down off Fortress Mountain through the silvered snow-frozen February night, to spread like a chill wind from another world across Jubilee Basin and engulf the Creighton place like ice.

The wolf sound was still hanging in the air as the terrified child came pelting through the house for Lydia to sweep him up in her arms and carry him back inside.

Beautel stood motionless on the porch. That single hackle-raising howl had died away but now the whole basin was a-howl, furred throats giving tongue in response from every compass point until the whole night seemed to pulsate with the noise, trembling the trees and shaking snow from the leaves.

In the mountains, the cry of the wolves was as commonplace as bird-song, but this hunter had never experienced anything quite like this. It drove home to him in a very graphic way just how many killers prowled this place and the effect it was having on the inhabitants.

He stayed on until Louis was asleep again and Lydia was nodding by the fire.

Riding back under the moving skies, Beautel was sober and thoughtful. Up until now, and despite that breathlessly close encounter with the killer wolf which seemed to have somehow divined that he posed a serious threat, he had been regarding this whole affair as something of a change of pace and an adventure with the possibility of a big pay day at the end of it. He now realized it was much more than that. No, he had not been spooked by that feral chorus, but it did alert him to the magnitude of the wolf problem in Jubilee Basin.

Morning would find him up and about at the hotel long before first light, cooking breakfast, checking out his equipment, getting ready to go wolf-hunting.

★   ★   ★

The wolves ran silently, pink tongues lolling and tufted ears lying back over their heads. The snow cover was thinner here and although the hunted were covering the ground faster than they had been ten minutes earlier, the horsemen behind were closing the gap.

There were four wolves in the pack

and they had blood on their jaws. The hunters had surprised the predators feasting on the freshly killed carcass of a steer out back of the Jenkinson place at Dark Canyon. They had chased swiftly and skilfully since to cut the wolves off continuously from the sanctuary of the woods. The quarry didn't want to enter the dark-jawed canyon looming ahead but suddenly there was no choice. To veer away would bring them into range of the guns. There had been no shooting thus far but they knew the hunters had guns. They always had guns.

Despite Beautel's advantages of youth, quality of horseflesh and determination, as the two horsemen stormed through a drift to send snow flying thirty feet into the air, his ancient companion managed to stay ahead as he'd done ever since the pursuit began.

Burns Wagons rode like a fifteen-year-old buck, with long legs wrapped around the ribcage of an aged mustang which could gallop like the undefeated champion of the entire Horse Nation.

Not that Beautel cared about being outridden by someone old enough to be his grandfather. They had the pack in their sights and that was all that counted as they went rushing into the canyon in pursuit, hoof echoes piling up between rearing walls of stone.

Bear Canyon was narrow but high-walled. The wolves were showing signs of anxiety as the going twisted and turned, for this was a region they avoided normally, since the only way out, once inside, was to climb the precipitous walls.

But the hunters were drawing closer. Suddenly one animal desperately broke away and began scrabbling up a steep yellow rock face.

Smoothly Beautel whipped his Winchester from its scabbard, threw it to the shoulder and squeezed trigger.

Paralysed by the agony of a shattered spine, the wolf arced backwards and fell all the way down to lie as motionless as something that had never lived.

'One Bluecoat down!' shouted Burns Wagons, who liked to live with past glories.

'Yours next,' called Beautel, flinging him the rifle, which he caught dexterously, jacking a fresh shell into the chamber as the quarry ahead began to yap and snarl.

The wolves knew they were done for when directly ahead loomed a towering bulwark of granite which seemed to reach all the way to threatening clouds.

Wildly searching for an exit, but finding none, their ears were seen to lift and the hackles on their shoulders stood stiff. Beautel knew the signs. If they could not run they would fight. A hunter almost got to admire the wolf for its intelligence and fighting spirit, unless of course that wolf happened to be coming for his throat.

The Winchester thundered and a second animal went down, yipping and biting at its flank where the agony was centered.

Instantly the third wolf wheeled,

leapt momentarily high with forelegs moving in a swimming motion. Then it hit ground and came rushing back towards the horsemen, as the fourth opted for the walls.

Burns Wagons cut loose. But the attacking wolf was not maintaining a straight line. Deliberately so. It ducked and weaved, nimble as a mountain goat, barely seeming to touch rock as it flew on with that magical wolf silkiness, bullets hammering powder puffs from the stones all about it but none striking home.

The Dakota was working the lever too fast. The Winchester jammed. Burns Wagons promptly hurled the weapon aside and whipped out his knife, bristling with redskin machismo. The man appeared ready to fling himself off his mustang and take El Lobo on, *mano a mano*, when Beautel got his revolver working.

He didn't miss. In most such situations, you could not afford to miss as a man mostly only ever used a handgun in desperate situations. If this was not desperate, the size and savagery of the wolf made it at least dangerous. Beautel squeezed off three swift shots which bellowed out in one continuous rolling roar. The wolf somersaulted with a wild wail, sprang to its feet, took another slug through the chest and fell dead.

Sliding over the rump of his mustang, Burns Wagons started back at a run to get the rifle. Ahead, one wolf was dying and the other was two hundred feet up the sloping north wall, clawing its way for the tree line over a surface it would find impossible to surmount except with death licking at its heels.

The sixgun recoiled against Beautel's thumb as he dispatched two slugs after the sole survivor. A sudden white scar appeared in dark stone thirty feet below the climber, the second slug slapping closer but still short.

Bramm!

The reassuring thunder of the Winchester filled Bear Canyon. Burns

Wagons had got his rifle working again. Slowly Beautel pushed the bay towards the dying wolf, fingering fresh shells into the chambers as his hunting partner loosed off another volley of shots at an ever-diminishing target.

Beautel reined in as the climber yelped. The wolf was hanging on, crimson showing on its hindquarters. Burns Wagons began to stomp and hoot, executing his victory dance.

He should have kept shooting.

Recovering in a moment, the wolf scrabbled up over the final reach of stone before the Indian could throw rifle to shoulder, then was gone with the farewell flick of a gray tail, leaving blood in its tracks.

The wounded wolf stared at Beautel implacably, hating him as only wolves can hate, hating him fiercely as the final bullet smashed its brain.

Beautel got down to build a cigarette while the Dakota went about with his knife taking the scalps that would fetch twenty bucks apiece in bounty in the town.

Beautel had slain a number of wolves since his arrival but had turned all the scalps over to Burns Wagons to claim. The old man had no funds, just a rich treasury of memories and a bitter hatred of, not wolves but horse-hunters. He could use the money. Beautel had made a vow on coming here not to settle for any tawdry little profits along the way until he stood up in Hardesty and the mayor handed him $500 for a huge black scalp with a silver blaze running down the face.

The big question, so he was telling himself as he leaned against his horse listening to its heavy breathing, was whether that big day was drawing any closer.

His gray gaze scanned the canyon and the dirty sky above.

They had accounted for three wolves.

On their ride out that morning, they had heard the latest party of hunting hopefuls, three hairy men from Montana, blasting away with everything they had off in the direction of Skyline Plateau.

The Montanans had a likely look about them and it figured that all that expended firepower suggested at least some kills.

Ranchers, towners, hunters and sporting shooters were rubbing out wolves in big numbers. Yet every time you turned around there were just as many. Last night at the Creighton place they'd almost deafened him, howling from one end of the basin to the other.

The irony was that men were hunting Deerkiller and killing other wolves in the process. Sightings of the man-killer were rare, but everyone knew he was out there. That first unforgettable howl last night had emanated from the throat of a big, barrel-chested Western timber wolf; nobody could have any doubts about that.

Maybe the killer was singing because he seemed invincible, Chet reflected. He mainly kept low, chose his own targets, and while he rested, hid or calmly schemed out his next attack, left it to his army of lesser wolves to man the barricades.

'Four,' smirked the redskin, returning with three dripping scalps.

'I'll wager you used the same brand of mathematics to tally all those wagons you say you set afire. It's three.'

'Fourth hurt bad, will soon die. Shot in hips. Can not chase game, so will perish. Four.'

Beautel squinted at the man through tobacco smoke.

'Tell me about the wagons.'

A born exhibitionist, Burns Wagons closed his eyes and chanted several bars of a Dakota war song. Then the imperious eyes snapped open and Beautel saw the fire there, banked but still burning.

'They wagon-riders steal our ponies.' He thumbed his scrawny chest. 'Many ponies. They leave us afoot and even braves are weeping. But I followed thieves for eleven days and nights until they no longer afraid. They were cruel with our ponies and two were already dead. They make circle at night with horses and our ponies in middle. In darkness I cut throats of two sentries and take white man's oil to soak the sleeping wagons . . . set them afire. They scream as they burn.'

Beautel stared. The bronzed face seemed to shine as though touched by an inner firelight. He believed the tale. It was impossible not to. He might have asked more but decided he had heard enough.

'It's always been horses with you, hasn't it, old man?'

'Horse is life. It is the wind and thunder, the rushing in the blood of young and old.' The Chief nodded. 'Bad men do bad things to good horses. So do horse-hunters here. This night fifty mustangs fret in town corrals. Hunters go chasing the wild ones while we chase the wolves. They have no heart. Man who will harm a horse is not man. One day I will — '

He broke off. From far distance came

the flat report of a single shot. Another wolf dead?

'Let's ride and talk, Chief.'

'Already we talk.'

'I mean about wolves,' Beautel grunted, filling leather. 'How come so many? Give me your theory. I know you've got one, like you have on everythin' else.'

It was true. Burns Wagons could be garrulously opinionated on matters as far-ranging as politics, miscegenation or the correct way to hone an axe. He had more knowledge of horses than anyone Chet had known.

But Jubilee Basin's self-replenishing wolf population had the Indian totally confounded. His best guess was that their profusion was the work of the Great Spirits; that they were sending a plague of wolves to punish people who made their living snaring wild horses.

Seemed Beautel would have to solve the mystery of the wolves himself.

5

The Sleeping Giant

The day Beautel and the old red man went hunting was officially the third day of spring, although it was doubtful if many in the troubled basin were aware of this fact.

Down in the lower country around Milltown it was a little warmer and merchants watched the skies, trying to decide if it was time to shift the fur coats and sturdy woollens from the show windows and replace them with something a little more summery.

Up along Rush River, which flowed down from its source in the Cascades around Fortress Mountain to make its way down through Ramont Valley, the official advent of the new season, even if it might be just as cold and snow-locked as winter up there, dominated every man's thoughts.

Spring was the time timbermen ceased pretending to be fully occupied and actually got busy. They wanted to see their holding ponds packed solid with cut logs awaiting release into the Rush to be borne downstream to the sawmen eagerly awaiting their arrival at Milltown.

Yet the ponds remained near empty, skeleton axe crews combed over the blighted slopes for anything overlooked in last season's felling frenzy, and in his fire-warmed quarters Ramont sat at his desk staring bleakly up at the lofty ridge separating his desolated valley from pristine, verdant and tree-rich Jubilee Basin.

The basin, where a huge black wolf dreamed in a high-roofed cavern at the far north end while a lesser wolf limped towards its death in the tall forests above Bear Canyon to the south.

The light in the forests that day was bitterly pale. It was bright but without warmth and winter still laid its dead hand on the silver of the ash and the snow-heavy bare birches and soaring pines. Here the oak trees sported their faded hues of gray-green moss, fringed by rusty brown.

Soon the snow would begin to melt and the cycle of growing and greening would begin again. Yet despite the harshness of the season now slowly passing there was sustenance to be foraged for beneath the snow for those deer brave enough to venture down from the relative safety of starving Skyline Plateau.

In the sifting light before the yawning mouths of the red rock caves, all locked in frosted silence, the golden stag stood listening to something moving through the trees.

It was a long way from the plateau and the stag had come alone. It was a young eight-pointer, already with its own extensive harem, strong and arrogant in its power, yet wary as every living creature must be in the basin.

Earlier the stag had gone to ground

at the muffled sound of shots lifting from the yawning gash of the canyon, had waited hidden a long time before venturing from the frozen brush again.

Now it swung about, poised for flight as the first drift of scent hit its quivering black muzzle.

There was but one smell like this and it was the smell of the whole basin. Wolf smell.

Up on the plateau, deer were gaunt-ribbed and half-starving, for the basin had grown too dangerous to visit, those few which dared often never returning. The stag was young and proud but anything but foolish. A wolf meant death, even to a powerful eight-pointer with its own string of pretty does.

The wolf appeared and the stag's muscles quivered beneath its golden hide as it readied to explode away.

But slowly the tension left lean legs and arched neck as the gray shape slumped in the snow to bite feebly at its hindquarters where red blood showed.

The stag's ears pricked sharply and its eyes riveted upon the wolf as it lurched forward again. It was dragging its hind legs, leaving furrows in the snow. The savage face crinkled into a ferocious snarl when it sighted the stag. But it mounted no charge. It could not.

At first the stag merely stood its ground, still shivering from the proximity of a lethal enemy, yet excited in a very different and combative way.

This was the ancestral enemy and it was injured, perhaps mortally so.

That first step the stag took towards the wolf was the most daring of its life. The wolf lifted its head and growled a warning. The stag sprang back a pace, but then pressed forward again. One step, two, three. It was closing in and all the enemy could do was grimace and growl as it dragged its agony over the white earth.

Quite suddenly, the stag attacked, lancing in with lowered head to bring its antlers sweeping close. It missed. It sprang back and the wolf tried to lunge, but lost balance. In a moment the stag was upon it, reaching the gray flank this time, hooking and ripping. The wolf howled in agony, snapped at a slender leg but missed by inches.

Torn between bravado and prudence, the excited stag continued to attack and retreat, attack and retreat, until the wolf was groaning in exhaustion, rolling its head this way and that until its gaze fell upon the dark cavern mouths close by.

The caverns stank of bear and no wolf ever went near them at this time of year. But when a raking antler ripped its side flesh again, the wolf snarled ferociously to drive its attacker back, then half-climbed, half-slithered up and over the stone apron and vanished within the largest cave.

The stag followed as far as the mouth. It was the last thing the wolf expected it to do. Driven deeper into the gloom, the crippled beast suddenly lost its footing and dropped through dark space to land on something soft, warm and growling. The awakening grizzly killed the intruder with one sweeping blow, its rage awesome at being awakened.

The stag vanished.

Now the bear grew aware of the thin lemon light filtering in and roared deafeningly and angrily because spring had come so early.

Immediately the four-month hunger struck like fangs gnawing its vitals, and still half-blind and confused from winter sleep, the monster began climbing towards the light.

* * *

The three Montanans swaggered along the main street of Hardesty as though they owned it. At midday the hunters had brought in two wolf-scalps and acted as though they expected the brass band to be dragged out of winter mothballs to welcome them, and the mayor to hand over the keys to his town.

Instead the mayor was locked up in

his dingy office discussing serious business with a visitor who, in the interests of prudence and privacy, had parked his carriage and entourage in back.

The Montanans had composed a hunting song about Deerkiller. It was a poor composition, the lyrics glaringly detached from reality. Lesser wolves had fallen to their trusty rifles and the man-killer would be next, or so their lyrics insisted as they clattered into the dry-goods store to inspect its line of big traps in which they were interested. They were looking for something real big.

Looking on, Hardesty sniffed and shrugged. Of course the citizenry were grateful that there were now two less wolves to worry about, five altogether counting the scalps Burns Wagons and Beautel had brought in earlier. But experience had taught the town that merely killing wolves had little if any bearing on the situation regarding Deerkiller.

Lesser wolves, much like the wolf-hunters themselves, came and eventually went. But Deerkiller merely vanished from the scene of one murderous attack and reappeared at the next, season after season, year after year.

The Montanans would learn this if they lived long enough. But in the meantime Hardesty went about its business, buying, selling, working and watching. An official twenty-four hour look-out was maintained from the flag-tower atop the hotel and armed citizens patrolled the perimeters even by daylight.

Hardesty was a war zone and its citizens were beginning to resemble the besieged of Atlanta. Nobody got enough rest, constant worry frayed nerve ends, some drank too much and others fought. Any period of relative calm was sooner or later shattered by a new disaster or a fresh attack, on this you could rely. People discussed the wolf plague in bemusement and the man-killer with fear and loathing. So some fool had killed Deerkiller's mate and cubs. How was it possible for a sensible person to believe any dumb animal would remember such a thing so long and pursue a systematic vendetta of retribution as a result? What would happen if all wild creatures acted that way? The West would empty out overnight — or just maybe, maybe the people of Jubilee Basin would still stand fast, even then.

They were proud people who still held their heads high.

They'd resisted Ramont's pressure to sell their timber leases even though God knew how badly they needed the income. They had likewise refused to budge when Deerkiller continued to haunt them, had even learned to cope when some weird abberation of Mother Nature had resulted in their being overrun by wolf-packs over the past year.

A siege mentality prevailed here, and it was their strength and pride. Jubilee against the Rest. Good riddance to the weak sisters who cracked, sold up and left. The town was better off without them. What was left was pure gold. They were true pioneer stock.

'They're a bunch of morons,' insisted Max Ramont, viewing Hardesty from behind the closed windows of the mayor's office suite. 'Some of these bigger landholders could retire on the fees I'd pay for relieving them of their surplus timber. Then they could afford to hire half Wyoming to get rid of their wolves. They like being losers.'

'Not like us, eh, Max?'

Mayor Horatio Buckner was small, nasal, nondescript. But he was also the town's premier businessman and would be far wealthier if only his voters would open the floodgates and allow Ramont Lumber to move holus bolus from the valley to the basin and start right in lopping anything standing over ten feet tall.

The horse-trading mayor was pro-logging, pro-Ramont and anti-conservation. He had made his money in the wild-horse trade, and at that moment, in the Double Forty corral out back of the building, had thirty odd horses eating him out of house and home while he waited to see whether Ramont would get his way here. Should logging commence in the basin, Ramont would need every mustang he could get, for the tough little wild horses were as essential to his operations as were the big percherons. The demand for horses would be ongoing and Ramont had already promised the mayor top dollar plus for his horses the day he succeeded in persuading Hardesty to change its mind.

Had Ramont been given a free hand here there would now be a few fresh graves, some shot-up buildings, a reasonable number of burnt-out ranch houses, and a huge Ramont Lumber sign erected atop the highest point in town, the tower room at the hotel.

Ramont liked to do business with fist and gun, which was largely the method by which he had over-taken his valley two seasons ago.

Such methods had earned him a small fortune and a great number of enemies, the most formidable of these being Sheriff Henley, the strongman peace officer of Milltown who had publicly vowed to jug the timber tycoon and throw away the key if he ever attempted to muscle his way into the basin.

The sheriff was hickory-tough and mule-stubborn. Any man had to be to bluff Ramont. County jail was crowded with powerful figures such as the timberman who'd sought to impose his own will upon this tract of the West. Offered the choice of life with either the sheriff or the killer wolf, Ramont would choose Deerkiller every time.

So now the big man was here again looking to fire up the mayor into imposing his authority and implementing the pro-lumber change of heart amongst the citizenry, all fair, square and almost legal.

'They should have folded by this,'

Ramont said in bitter frustration, watching the tense street again. 'I've got them running scared, locking their houses all day long, sleeping with rifles instead of women and jumping six feet every time a dog barks. What does it take to crack a hick town anyway?'

The mayor stared at his guest solemnly. He was not sure he understood what Ramont meant concerning ' . . . by this'. He had the uneasy feeling he was better off not knowing.

* * *

Beautel leaned in the doorway of the dry-goods store watching the Montanans skylarking around with their traps. He wanted to get moving, having just heard Lydia Creighton was in town, visiting friends from the church, so he understood. But this noisy trio was bothering him. Decent folks were hurting and even dying here, yet these wolvers acted like it was just all a big game to them, a game that would eventually result with their accounting for Deerkiller, claiming the bounty money, and having a bunch of hick towners kissing their hands in gratitude.

Maybe it was time someone had a quiet word.

The trio was headed his way with the biggest wolf trap in the store, a steel jawed monster four feet long.

'That killer can't be trapped by one of those things,' he stated bluntly.

They halted.

'Well, if it ain't the cookin' champ mountain man,' smirked the scrawny one. He tapped a companion on the shoulder. 'This is him, Hermie, the hot-shot everyone's wagerin' their money on to bring this big old wolf back in a sack. But how long's he been here? And do you see any sign of any killer hangin' out to dry? Do you, huh?'

All laughed. They were raw-boned denizens of the wild trails with rough manners and dirty hands. They looked like huntsmen but that didn't necessarily make them so in Beautel's eyes.

'When a wolf reaches a certain age,' he stated, 'he's past fallin' for traps. He gets so he can smell the steel, can pick out a set at fifty yards on a dark night. They'll tell you here that Deerkiller hasn't set off a single trap or gone within a mile of a poisoned bait in years. So he's not likely to slip back into bad habits just to oblige you fellers, is he?'

They were attracting passers-by, amongst them several hunters who were making peanuts with the twenty-dollar bounties and slowly giving up hope of ever bagging the man-killer. These men had come to regard Beautel as something special despite the fact he'd enjoyed no greater success than themselves thus far. The Montanans were aware of this and resented it. For they were the tops — in their own minds, at least.

'Man oh man, but we're just an ignorant bunch of rubes, ain't we,' jeered the largest, the one with the huge trap slung over his shoulder. He was playing to the audience. 'Any more tips, Long Hair? We'd be real grateful.'

'Just one,' said Beautel quietly, hitching at his belt. 'No, maybe two. But this one's important.' He pointed. 'A trap that size could take off a man's leg, and from what I've seen of you pilgrims you mightn't know where to set it where there's no risk of catchin' someone.'

The Montanans had stopped smirking. They were getting sore.

'And what's the other tip?' challenged the third, a slit-eyed redhead with jug ears. 'C'mon, mountain man, you been so generous you might as well give us the lot.'

Beautel tried to bite his tongue. He had important matters demanding his attention and had no inclination to tangle with anyone right now. Yet he found he couldn't hold back.

'OK,' he said, heaving himself off the doorframe. 'Seems to me you could do everybody a good turn by headin' back to Montana. You ain't goin' to catch the killer. You got two wolves today but shot a heifer in the process. All you're doin' is stirrin' things up and these folks can do without that.'

He saw the swinging trap coming at him from the corner of his eye. He ducked and drove a shoulder into the big man, driving him clear off his feet. He backed up nimbly as the others came at him. He didn't want to fight, couldn't see it would gain anything. The towners in the street were urging him on but he continued to back-pedal until the redhead rushed him, diving low to try and take him around the middle. Beautel swayed aside, rabbit-punched to the back of the neck and gave the Montanan a taste of boot leather on his way down.

'Mr Beautel! Really!'

He recognized the voice. He swung to see Lydia and Louis watching from a short distance away. Then something hard bounced off his jaw and he was seeing stars. Cursing now, angry for the first time, he exploded into a flurry of fists and elbow smashes, drawing blood and quickly leaving no doubt in anyone's minds that the Montanans really were rubes when it came to rough-housing.

It was all over in seconds, yet the Creightons were gone before he could get free of the back-slappers crowding about him. He eventually caught up with the pair down at the assembly hall, where the mayor had called an unscheduled meeting to discuss the 'crisis' confronting his community.

Beautel found a seat beside Lydia, but she remained aloof. He had almost established himself as a gentleman out at the farm, he knew, yet the woman's icy silence now told him what she thought of public brawling — all the more so on a day when, as the runty mayor kept stating from the podium, they were in crisis.

With no alternative, Beautel sighed and sat through the remainder of the meeting in silence, during which time he gained the clear impression that the

Hardesty man and woman in the street were slowly but surely running out of endurance.

He caught sideways glances directed his way and knew that his accounting for three and perhaps four wolves that morning had impressed but briefly. Everyone knew the predators seemed to breed like jack rabbits. And there hadn't even been a single sighting recently of Deerkiller to encourage them to believe any real progress was being made.

'Long Hair' had let them down and the Montanans had lost all credibility. That was the pervading mood. Then suddenly there was Max Ramont himself mounting the podium to restate his 'more than generous' offer on their timberlands which could haul Jubilee out of its doldrums overnight.

Lydia was on her feet trying to rally the anti-logging forces when Beautel quit the hall to make his way south along the street.

Despite his lack of success he

remained confident of achieving what he'd come here to do. In time. But that was the crux. There was a feeling that time was running out both for himself and the basin.

By the time he reached the hotel he had decided to go night-hunting. This could prove risky, especially when dealing with a critter like this killer. But he had done it before and was confident he could more than hold his own against any damn wolf.

He wanted that critter. But even more, he wanted to reinstate himself in Lydia's good graces, and wasn't too proud to admit it. He liked kids and refined women, but of course nothing ever went any farther than that. Not when freedom was your god, it didn't.

★   ★   ★

It was Big Julie of the Chinook saloon who heard it first. She was a poor sleeper and was in the habit of sitting up in bed nights reading romantic pulpers about French counts and nubile serving maids until drowsing off.

Her first thought was that a brawl had erupted somewhere in town, for there was a slamming, thudding pattern about the sounds that had a familiar ring to the ears of a girl reared in rough-house saloons. Then she heard a strange roaring, like an angry bull giving tongue, and wondered if perhaps Chicken Pickle's prize Hereford had somehow gotten loose and was cutting up rough.

The buxom girl rose and padded to her window. Hardesty lay wrapped in fog with just four dim street-lamps visible. For a minute there was nothing to be seen, and the sounds weren't repeated. But next instant she was backing away from the window with one hand to her throat as the 'monster' emerged from the alley alongside the general store.

There was nothing wrong with Big Julie's lungs, just her sleeping habits. She screamed at full volume and

Hardesty was jolted rudely awake, certain it must be the killer wolf as they fumbled for rifles in the dark and bumped into one another as they tried to get to see what was happening on the street.

'An ogre!' another half-awake citizen howled, and indeed so it appeared through the fog and the gloom. But in reality it was a bear, a hurting, raging giant jolted prematurely from hibernation, driven to lumber down out of the high country in desperate search of food, only to blunder into a trap set to snare a wolf.

The Montanans had attached the trap's eight feet of heavy chain to an oak-log drag which the bear was throwing and slamming about in a red fury.

Yet these facts weren't immediately evident to many, and there was genuine terror in the town as men snatched up guns and went running into the streets. Many of these people had had first-hand experiences with wolf attacks, some had even lost kin to Deerkiller's murderous marauding. Children screamed and women fought to calm them as the bear continued on its rampage, swinging its body this way and that, the chain and drag-log snapping behind it like the tail on a kite.

The log snared frequently and the bear would haul remorselessly on its chain, then give up and go back to tear it free. Once he lifted it and held it tenderly for a moment, like a baby. Then he dropped it and rushed furiously away until the log caught between a lamppost and a hitch rail, snapping it to a violent halt again. The animal went insane and threw all its power on to the chain which snapped taut and broke the hitching rail in a single snap.

Next moment it was hit.

Nobody knew who fired the shot; there were many men with guns on the street by this time. All saw the red-and-white flare of the bear's gaping jaws as it screamed in pain, and there was panic as it started back toward the men, only to veer abruptly off down a side street, the chinking, thudding sound of the drag-log fading away into silence within a very few seconds.

From the balcony of the hotel where he was staying overnight following the long meeting, Ramont looked down on a town in shock.

The fact that the nightcomer had not been the killer wolf seemed immaterial at the moment. Indeed, the slow-dawning comprehension that this was some new threat to their peace of mind appeared to hit the townspeople harder for that very fact. It was as if they felt that they were being singled out by fate to suffer whatever disaster the wind might blow in. A mad bear crashing through town in the middle of the night. What next? Tornadoes? A small-pox epidemic?

Ramont drew a cigar from the breast pocket of his brocaded robe, his face taut with excitement. He'd played no part in the incident of the bear yet sensed that in its random way it might prove to be the straw which broke the camel's back. Hardesty tonight acted and sounded like a place teetering on the edge of collapse and surrender. For the logger king, the timing could not have been better.

6

Bloody Spring

'Too many horses,' declared Burns Wagons, toasting his toes at the fire, his expression taut with concentration. 'Always many fine ponies caged like dogs until mayor sells. But this time he does not sell. This time more horses than ever. Yards are full, yet still hunters bring them in and still evil mayor does not sell. Why so?'

'Only an Indian,' Lydia observed sardonically, 'could possibly fret about a bunch of mustangs in a corral after the week we've just had. The bear barging into town like that would alone be enough to divert anyone half-way normal, which I'm afraid casts some serious doubts about your friend, Chet.'

'My friend?' Beautel objected, eying the sprawled figure hogging all the fire.

'That's too big a word, Lydia. A sidekick at best. He's a scalper at heart and still a sworn enemy of both the United States of America and horse-hunters everywhere. Folks don't make friends with people like that, not even long-haired mountain men.'

They were trying to insult the Chief to get him off the subject of his horses, but without success. Resting up at the spread with Beautel *en route* back to Hardesty following an unsuccessful search for the suffering bear, Burns Wagons might have been all alone, so intent was he on his analysis of the horse mystery, which from his biased viewpoint, outweighed all others.

He rambled on. Lydia set about dressing a gash to Beautel's hand, while Louis was at at the lamplit table smiling over his neglected homework.

For the boy, Beautel's arrival in the basin was the best thing to have happened since his father disappeared. He loved his mother but she had become too serious, critical and complaining under the stress of keeping the place going, raising a child alone and now coping with the wolf menace.

Until the mountain man showed, that was.

Chet had changed most everything, from Louis's point of view.

At first the child was certain his mother had disapproved of the tall man with his buckskins and great mane of hair, had once actually heard her describe him as 'exactly the breed one might rely on to make any situation worse rather than better.'

Lydia didn't say things like that any more and Louis was overjoyed when Beautel began stopping by the spread in such a friendly way. The boy was especially pleased with tonight's visit as he had a half-hunch the wolf hunter might remember it was his birthday.

Beautel had indeed remembered. Only thing, having spent the past sixteen hours searching for the bear to put it out of its misery, there had been no opportunity to get the kid a present.

Nevertheless he didn't intend allowing the occasion to pass unmarked. This was a harsh environment and a tough life for any kid. Beyond the four walls of this frame-house lurked enough trouble, danger and uncertainty to age a child ahead of his time, so he was determined to bring a little joy, if possible.

When Louis was diverted by yet another Burns Wagons outburst against all men who did not love horses as he did, Beautel drew the woman aside and produced his worn leather billfold.

'Somethin' for the boy,' he said. 'Only got notes. Okay by you?'

Lydia nodded. Seated straight-backed at the head of the table, she was not her usual self tonight. She was glum and mostly silent, and held the bear responsible. Many a basin citizen tonight shared her feelings.

The bear incident seemed like the last straw.

Somehow she'd been able to cope

with the Deerkiller menace mainly because she'd always noted that the lobo rarely bothered anyone who didn't bother it first.

The wolf infestation of the past year had however proved far more threatening, so much so that in recent months she'd seriously considered quitting the basin, this despite the fact that she'd always vowed to remain until either she received official confirmation of her husband's death, or he returned.

Now men were setting traps all over the basin and catching by mistake bears that terrorized the country. How much could a person take?

Her visitors had brought the news that the bear incident was already having far-reaching effects throughout the valley. Valley folk were now seriously questioning Hardesty's ongoing community ban on logging in the basin. It was rumored that several landholders might now give up, sell their timber leases to Ramont and quit 'Wolf Basin'. Folks could only take so much.

So why should a thirty-year-old farming woman with calluses on her hands and a genuine fear of seeing her long fight against the pro-lumber faction in the basin end in final defeat feel irritated because someone wanted to give her son a birthday present?

She already knew why. Someone should offer her a gift, she thought with guilty selfishness. She had not had one single present since losing her husband. Her last birthday had been marked only by a pack of wolves killing their best heifer out behind the sump.

She pulled herself together and forced a smile. Of course Chet could do as he wished, she said. He flipped his billfold open. Lydia Creighton could not help but stare at the sight of a fat wad of large-denomination banknotes.

Maybe she should have refrained from commenting but was too exhausted and envious not to do so.

'I suspected as much from the first day I saw you, Chet,' she said. 'You are not really interested in the bounty at all, are you. Obviously you don't need that bounty. It really irks me when people are less than candid, you know. But seeing as I'm now aware you have money, as a friend would you be so good as to tell me the real reason you came to the basin.'

'Would if I could,' he answered casually, flicking his hair back off his shoulders.

Her dark brows creased. 'In other words, you won't tell me.'

'I came here to get that killer, Lydia, and I still mean to do that. But like you figure, there was another reason that saw me quit on my pards and the big money in the Rockies. I guess I was startin' to feel that I was tryin' to be somethin' I could never be. I mean, you know . . . hard-workin' and respectable I guess you'd call it.'

'Well I never!' she said crossly. 'Imagine fearing respectability.' Lydia might have said more but at that moment her son noticed the tip of a crumpled bill concealed in Beautel's fist.

Chet saw the boy's look, grinned, snapped his hand open. Nothing there. A laughing Louis turned it over and Lydia gasped as he plucked the twenty-dollar bill from between Beautel's fingers.

'Oh no, Chet,' Lydia protested, 'that's far too much. I can't allow you to be so generous.'

But he just shrugged and rose from the table, restless and edgy now as he made his cat-footed way for the door.

Outside in the bone-cracking cold of a brilliant starry night, the mountain man was prey to impatience as he listened to the eerie howling cascading down over the wooded tiers to the rangelands.

It was true he'd come here for the reasons just stated. He'd anticipated a tough hunt but was unprepared for the mysteries piling atop complexities that he'd encountered. He was convinced he could still bag Deerkiller given half a chance to concentrate on the killer and its hunting range. This, however, was proving impossible, frustratingly so.

The young wolves so confused the sign that expert huntsmanship was simply not possible. They were killing stock and getting shot and occasionally claiming a human victim, while Deerkiller was rarely even sighted, much less threatened.

Abruptly the wolves fell silent and the whole night was hushed until the door burst open behind him and the Chief emerged now, hunched up to his chin in a neck-to-ankle black buffalo-hide cape and munching on a chunk of apple pie, courtesy of their hostess.

'Come, Long Hair, we go free ponies.' He pounded Chet vigorously on the back, having downed half a bottle of Lydia's rosemary wine by the fire. 'Tonight is night they must be freed, otherwise great herds of sacred horses will not carry Burns Wagons to his place in sky when he dies of pneumonia at sixty-four.'

Amongst the Indian's preoccupations, chief of which was his passion for the wild ponies, was his total conviction that he would die of pneumonia. He'd always believed this, which was one of the main reasons he had shown such contemptuous disregard for the bullets of both his redskin and Bluecoat enemies during his days of war. He knew he would die in bed. Coughing and sipping whiskey. Aware of the Dakota's stubbornness and iron determination, Beautel wouldn't be at all surprised if he did die as he predicted when his time came. He was too ornery not to.

Not that he was much interested one way or the other. Nor — or so he told himself — was he concerned about why he continued to visit the Creightons the way he did. Times, a man could do too much thinking.

He'd done all that and was getting no place fast.

Now he was ready to get serious and stay in the saddle until he'd accounted for Deerkiller — the job he'd undertaken.

He would scout faster, farther and more intelligently than ever before if that was what it took to solve the mystery of the wolf packs and bring Deerkiller's pelt back in a calico sack.

Drifter's pride.

A drifter's do-or-die spirit.

He felt reinvigorated as he boasted to Burns Wagons that he would come back having achieved both goals or might not be back at all. Then he lashed the bay away across the frozen slopes leaving an admiring yet puzzled Dakota staring after him.

'Long Hair even crazier than Chief!' he grunted admiringly, blowing gusts of fog breath. 'That take heap plenty doing.'

The Chief was always impressed by erratic behaviour. Even so, as he headed for Hardesty astride his gaunt-ribbed mustang, he had soon cleared Beautel, the wolves and even the handsome ranch woman's apple pie from his thoughts and was concentrated again on all his beautiful sad 'brothers', locked up like criminals in the mayor's corrals.

He believed Beautel was now as obsessed with his wolves as he himself was with his wild horses. The Chief nodded in full approval of them both. He'd always believed that if a man committed himself to something he should go all out.

And wondered if they would survive their obsessions. For none knew better than Burns Wagons that this was highly dangerous country, with or without the wolves.

* * *

At last the deer were growing scarce in the basin as the calendar said spring but the bite in the air still proclaimed winter.

It had always been the custom of the deer from higher up on Skyline Plateau to delay being forced down into either the valley or the basin for as long as possible because of the dangers there.

The deer ranged widely over the plateau until the final six to eight weeks of the snow season found them half-starved and weakening after every last cedar was browsed up beyond reach and nothing worth foraging for was to be found beneath the snow.

So they reluctantly ventured down to the grasslands as they had done over countless generations, but this season it was different. The high valley was no longer the timbered haven it had once been but had been transformed during the summer by men with guns and traps and screaming machines into a dangerous hellscape into which only the most desperate animal would venture.

This left only the basin.

The basin offered as ample grazing and foraging as it had ever done, yet it too had become a danger-ground for the deer to which only the menace of starvation could have driven them.

For this season, when all hungry deer were concentrated in the basin, was also the year of the wolf. Not Deerkiller, who'd earned his name at their expense. The great timber wolf rarely ate deer any more, preferring to kill men's cattle and horses for sustenance as well as to compound the terror. But the huge increase in wolf numbers had placed the stags, does and yearlings at great peril: they had no choice. Come to the basin or perish.

And perish they did. But such were the wolf numbers now, that those which were not shot, baited or trapped, could never find enough deer and were forced to attack the landholders' livestock.

The packs made repeated incursions into the cattle- and sheep-herds, decimated the goats, murdered fine horses when they could, were not averse to gobbling up chickens, geese and ducks and left many a farm or ranch yard a grisly, feathered slaughterhouse by dawn's early light.

They were aided by the fact that, apart from the professional bounty hunters haunting the basin now in search of Deerkiller, the valley men who'd earlier formed wolf-hunting posses had all but quit. The presence of so many ravenous wolves in a limited region created a natural atmosphere of fear. Hunting the packs was a dangerous game which was compounded every now and then when the killer would emerge from his snowy fastnesses to take out some luckless hunter, sending every 'wolf-hunter' scurrying back to spread or town.

It was vaguely agreed now that the only logical explanation of the wolf numbers was the same kind of ecological mishap responsible for mouse or locust plagues.

In the meantime the basin grew poorer by the week, yet still the ranchers held out, refusing to allow Ramont to bring his brawling axemen and stinking engines into Jubilee and reduce it to the desolation that was now Ramont Valley.

Upon his favorite look-out spot at the high end of the basin, the great wolf saw it all through hooded eyes; watched the eager young wolves running down the deer in the snow and calmly observed the men who dared come out this far, travelling in groups with all their weapons.

If Deerkiller puzzled over the explosion in the numbers of his brothers and sisters he showed no sign. For he was still the wolf king and there was not a single young dog wolf, even those blooded in action and in their natural prime, which dared do anything but whimper and slither away should he suddenly appear on his big, black-nailed paws, his slanted yellow eyes glittering with a wisdom and an authority none dared challenge.

Occasionally even now, after all the lonely years, the man-killer would visit the place known as Marmot Hollow way back in the Fastness Ranges where it had all happened long ago.

That spring Deerkiller gambolled through the trees with his pretty bride, hunted swiftly and successfully to feed the two fat cubs concealed in the caves above the hollow.

The hunter he killed when the man drew too close to the den was his first. The man who died was rich and influential, and soon there appeared a famous hunter who was clever and cunning, who successfully trapped the she-wolf during Deerkiller's absence, the little ones drowning in the streamlet when drawn from their cave by the bitch's dying cries.

Deerkiller tracked the famous hunter into the main street of Hardesty by his scent and tore out his throat in front of a hundred people before escaping without a bullet touching him.

Thus began the notoriety and the lonely years of killing. Until this day as the wolf sat staring downwards. But not staring at some inevitable tableau of pursuit and death, nor as witness to the pathetic attempts made by the men to reclaim their basin from the new wolf plague. Rather Deerkiller watched two wolves at play in the snow, a male and female, nipping and skipping and occasionally raising their voices in song — telling him it really was spring even if he might have forgotten.

★ ★ ★

Tom Whiskey spat out a bloodied tooth which struck a metal beer tankard and ricocheted off like a spent bullet. Instantly the grimed visitor to Milltown, who lent a whole new meaning to the term 'the great unwashed', snatched up a heavy bar stool and heaved it violently at his opponent, a bull-necked sawmiller with blood streaming from a chewed ear and one eye shut tight and already turning black.

The jack ducked and the stool sailed across the bar to take out an expensive mirror and two shelves of bottles.

That did it.

Now the saloonkeeper blew a shrill blast through his bosun's whistle he kept slung around his neck for use in emergencies, and his peacekeepers came running.

But even these toughs baulked on sighting Whiskey standing defiant at the bar, wild eyes blazing and huge hairy hands clutching a long rifle by the barrel, ready to swing.

'Come on, you namby-pamby sons of bitches!' he bellowed in a voice which shook spiders down from the rafters. 'If I can't take twenty of you then I'll take the habit and join a convent. Which girlie boy wants his skull caved in first?'

He drank a great deal but rarely in the towns. That was because he was the worst possible drunk and invariably wound up in trouble. He'd hit the hard stuff in Milltown today because his girl had rejected him. She was forty-five years of age and weighed more than he did. A venomous loner by nature, Tom Whiskey figured if he could not hold on to Ugly Alice then his hopes of getting a bride to join him up in the high lonesome with only critters for company had to be around zero.

So he drank. The brawling followed as naturally as night follows day, and it was only when the bartender daringly leaned across his counter and clobbered the hairy giant with a beer-keg bung, sending him wobbly-legged, that the bouncers dared move in.

Even so, it was still a hell of a fight, for even a dazed Whiskey was still as strong as a bear and capable of tossing two-hundred-pounders about like sacks of chaff, stoving up furnishings and setting the percentage girls screaming up a storm.

He was still on his feet but vastly the worse for wear when the law arrived.

The trouble ended right then and there. There were few men who intimidated Max Ramont's meat-shooter from the valley, but Sheriff Henley was one. Long, lean and humorless, Henley was a walking law book, a stickler for procedure and as formidable a man as ever rode the basin trails.

The sheriff hated Tom Whiskey and harbored suspicions about his connections with Ramont Valley. Nothing about the troublemaker hit the badgeman right.

He was convinced he was a crook but could never fit him with anything really serious, apart from the occasional drunk and disorderly. He found Whiskey secretive, sly, vicious and devious. And these were just his better qualities.

'Put down that rifle,' ordered the lawman, and Whiskey meekly obeyed. Then, 'Who started this, Herbie?'

Naturally it had been Whiskey. Which left the sheriff with his standard option:

'You can pay the damages or do thirty days in the — '

'I'll pay,' Whiskey panted. Then he added respectfully, 'Sheriff.'

Henley blinked. The saloon was half-wrecked.

'Two hundred dollars,' he rapped, ready to conduct his man to the slammer.

But Whiskey thrust a huge hand into the deep recess of his layered wardrobe to produce a vast fistful of money. The sheriff was peeved but had to accept it, for the law was the law and Tom Whiskey had paid up. But the lawman

151

was frustrated and cranky as he stiffly escorted the smirking trouble-maker along to the wagon yard where he'd kept his rig overnight. He'd love to hand this man thirty days. Even more, he'd like to know just how come a man who seemed to spend far more time raising hell than working, always appeared to be cashed up. He didn't buy the meat-shooter's role both Ramont and Whiskey claimed. They had real shooters up at the valley and this man was not one of them.

'One month,' Henley said tightly as Whiskey clambered up on to the seat of his strange rig. He sniffed at the smell. Whiskey stank of animals, as did his wagon which featured a stout wire canopy enclosing a space large enough to house a couple of grizzly bears. 'If I see you back here in that time I'll jug you, mister. And you can tell Ramont I'll be up to check on him before the week's out.'

'Yeah, right, Sheriff.' Whiskey's battered face was deliberately blank. 'Anythin' else?'

The badgeman stood at the curbside, hands on hips, eyes cut to slits. Whiskey merely disgusted him. But Henley had a real vendetta going with his boss. He suspected Ramont of coercion, intimidation, extortion, illicit business practices and enough offences to fill a full file at the jailhouse. His main goal in life was to nail the lumber king for something before his operation in the valley petered out entirely, but he didn't fancy his chances.

It was just possible Ramont was too clever for him. Just as it was conceivable that even hairy Tom Whiskey had his number, judging by the way he'd extricated himself from this latest scrape.

Such thoughts were bad for the sheriff's self-esteem, and he was excessively officious as he ordered Whiskey on his way, peevishly extending the period of his banishment from polite society from four weeks to eight.

Leaving an eye-watering stink in his wake, Whiskey nodded in grave submission; yet his brute eyes glittered brightly as he glanced back over his shoulder to see the tall figure still standing there, watching him go.

He was proud of himself today. He had not surrendered to his natural instincts and gone for the lawdog's throat, even though liquored up and almost out of control. He owed his 'self-discipline' to Ramont. The big man had finally convinced him that one big victory was worth a score of minor wins. And regardless of what had happened here today, and unmindful of his disappointment in the romance stakes, Tom Whiskey was keeping his eye fixed firmly on the main game.

They were close to seeing Jubilee Basin fall into their hands for logging, due less to Ramont's concentrated pressure than to Whiskey's secret contribution to breaking down the basin's resistance.

Small wonder Ramont paid him more than any man on his pay-roll, he reflected smugly. And when the basin hold-outs finally signed on the dotted line and Ramont Lumber moved into Jubilee, there would be the prize of a huge bonus for Whiskey which he'd richly earned.

He could afford to let Henley push him around. The last laugh would be his.

7

Face to Face

Beautel froze, staring at the sign at his feet.

He'd been tracking the dying bear afoot over a mile through high country too difficult for a horse to negotiate. It was a solemn part of the huntsman's creed, learned from his father in their early days together in the Rockies, never to allow a wounded animal to die in pain if it could be avoided. His plan today was to find and finish off the bear, then undertake a wide sweep across almost inaccessible country which lay in the rugged region between the south head of the basin and the mighty bulk of Fortress Mountain.

He told himself he would be searching for the elusive Deerkiller, yet knew he was more interested in uncovering some kind of explanation for the wolf packs. Now, standing motionless staring down at the snow, both wolves and bears suddenly became secondary. At this point, the dragging, blood-smeared prints of the bear had been overlaid by another set, those of a wolf. But this was no ordinary wolf. These were huge tracks identical with others he'd cut from time to time as he criss-crossed the basin in search of his killer.

Deerkiller's tracks.

The pug-marks were distinctive even apart from their size. Where lesser wolves were forced to cover great distances in their hunt for prey here in a place where competition for the dwindling deer grew more fierce every day, the predators' spoor showed toenails worn down and at times deformed by excessive activity. But the nails on these prints were long and strong. They told him this outsized wolf was so skilled at killing, so powerful and lethal, that it didn't even have to work hard to get all the food it wanted even at the dog-end of winter with game in short supply. His heart thudded with excitement as he lifted his gaze to see the solitary wolf's tracks following the bear's away between brush and trees into what appeared to be a steep-walled box canyon.

He listened and sniffed the air. His mountain man's senses easily identified the smell of bear and blood mingled with the pungent, musky aroma of wolf.

His hands were steady as he jacked a shell into his rifle. He moved on with infinite quietness to climb slowly through the snow-covered patches of open ground in amongst rocks and gnarled trunks. Now the box canyon began to open up before him, and moments later a faint flicker of movement caught his eye ahead and to the right.

He propped again.

Seated prettily on a knob of granite not fifty yards distant was a female gray wolf, her ears raised and pointed forwards. The she-wolf was watching something below her intently, until the wind changed fractionally. Beautel's scent hit her like a bullet and she was up and off, vanishing in just two or three impossibly fluent bounds, so swiftly that it was possible to doubt she had been there at all.

But Beautel had seen everything, knew for sure something was happening down below. He lunged forward with rifle at the ready. The first thing he saw from the granite knob was the great bear lying dead on the floor of the box, the foreleg by which it had been trapped almost torn away, the chain still connected to the drag-log.

Probably in darkness, the bear had fallen into the box and died. But the predator which had gone down after it to feed upon the carcass had obviously slid down a smooth stone slipway right at Beautel's feet, for this was the only way in or out of the steep-walled canyon.

And Deerkiller was charging up the stone chute towards him, the size of a pony, lips skinned back in a terrible snarl, those big healthy toenails somehow finding purchase on the smooth stone.

Beautel threw up the rifle and drew a bead on the face twenty yards beneath him. Instantly the wolf stopped as though already accepting the reality of its fatal error. It refused to whine or try to spin away. It simply crouched there staring up at him as if recognizing the inevitability of its death, accepting it as it studied the man responsible for ending its splendid journey, hating fiercely for the final time.

Slowly the rifle barrel came down and the man met the beast's stare levelly, experiencing feelings half-sensed before but never really recognized or understood. The wolf was the finest specimen the hunter had ever seen, the distillation of every wolf, stag, buffalo, beaver, bighorn sheep or mighty bull moose ever to come under his gun.

Seconds stalked the charged silence.

Chet had killed a dozen times since coming here, and all he had to do to register his biggest kill ever was jerk trigger.

One bullet.

He didn't do so.

How come?

The closest he could figure, was an overpowering sense of kinship with this animal he'd come to kill.

Chet Beautel was a man born to that free and unfettered way of life which he'd reclaimed on quitting the Beavertail Trappers. He was seeing this beast in front of him as some kind of brother of the blood, and what he was experiencing must have registered in his stance, his scent, or simply in the expression in his eyes.

Whatever the case, Deerkiller suddenly broke the silence with a soft growl, spun within its own length on the smooth surface of the slipway and went leaping back down the way it had come.

Beautel watched it go. He could have killed it a dozen times, but didn't fire a shot. A hundred feet below, Deerkiller paused to stare back with an expression akin to puzzlement. Somewhere close by, a wolf yipped sharply. The female. Deerkiller's black tufted ears pricked sharply at the sound but he did not unlock his eyes from the man's.

Whatever passed between them was indefinable yet powerful. The day of the mountain man drifter, like that of the great wolf, was swiftly passing. They were anachronisms in the day of the iron horse and swarming migration which was eating up all the wild and lonely places. The wolf was true to what it had always been, as was he. Both seemed to sense this at the same moment. Then the wolf turned and was gone, leaving the man grinning foolishly and thinking: maybe only somebody like Burns Wagons would understand something like this.

After a time, Beautel mounted and headed higher through the tumbled foothills of the mountain. He was no longer searching, merely riding while reflecting on his strange experience. But as is so often the case when a man is not looking for anything in particular, he found something. Something passing strange.

★ ★ ★

Sheriff Henley rode into Hardesty just on noon, boosted along the main street by a cold wind blustering down off Skyline Plateau.

Newsman Nathan Pooley, who saw him pass from his office window at the *Herald*, leaned back in his chair with a thoughtful frown and sucked on a pencil.

'You reckon the sheriff's heard, Mr Pooley?' asked his ink-stained typesetter, cleaning grubby hands on a swab of cotton waste.

'Sheriff Henley hears everything sooner or later, George.'

'He's a good man.'

'And a frustrated one.' The newspaperman heaved himself from his chair and reached for his hat. 'Like most of us this winter, I guess.'

'Spring, Mr Pooley.'

'Huh? Oh yes, so it is.' The editor and publisher of the *Basin Herald* paused to gaze from his windows at the slushy street a moment. 'Seems a man needs reminding of that fact this year for some reason. I mean, when one looks out to see nothing but snow, cold, and hard times, with the occasional tax collector or son of a bitch wandering by, just to depress you a little further, I guess spring still seems a long way away.'

'Any particular son of a bitch in mind, sir?' the typesetter asked curiously.

'I'll leave you to guess, George,' Pooley said, going out. 'Something the good newsman must learn to do is guess educated.'

George returned to his ancient Albion hand-press and reached for his type case to begin loading his type stick. He chewed his underlip thoughtfully for a moment, then nodded.

'Ramont. Yeah, that would be my educated guess, boss. I mean, he's rich, he's arrogant, he pushes folks around and he just happens to be in town today. Gotta be him.'

Had Max Ramont overheard this conversation at the office of a news organ he had every sound reason to detest, it would neither have impressed nor surprised him.

The Hardesty paper had been anti-logging from day one and had used its influence to deride his every effort to break down the basin's resistance to Ramont Lumber. It had even, from time to time, cast almost libelous aspersions on the region's most successful timberman.

Maybe Pooley, his lousy rag and all the righteous anti-progress nobodies who'd succeeded in keeping him out of the basin for far too long had a big payback coming their way, or so

Ramont often opined. He was the kind of man who never forgot or forgave.

But the Ramont who was at that moment making his relaxed way toward the assembly hall where today's vital debate was to be conducted, was drawing on his freshly lit Cuban and even smiled forgivingly at the handful of rugged-up citizens brandishing NO LOGGING posters whom he encountered along the sidewalks.

It was not that the big man had undergone any change of heart towards his enemies, detractors or poison-pen newspaper editors. No chance of that. Yet today he felt he could afford to be gracious in what smelt like the whiff of victory for his cause, namely a reversal of the town's former hard line against logging and loggers.

Ramont had always had his hard core of supporters in Hardesty, headed up by the town's avaricious and gutless little mayor. Unfortunately for the timberman's ambitions, the anti faction here had always heavily outweighed the pro, with many vocal and passionate people, such as Lydia Creighton, for example, helping to keep the citizens strong and united against him and his expansionary plans all over Hondo County.

Today Ramont sensed that the change he'd been so desperately seeking seemed to be almost at hand.

And it seemed he had a big dumb bear to thank.

Ramont had put his faith in wolves, yet when three dumb Montanans set a huge wolf-trap which had succeeded in snaring one cranky bear aroused from hibernation, that critter's violent rampage through the night streets of Hardesty had seemed to turn the tide his way. The incident had apparently had a last-straw effect on a community worn thin by adversity, and when he'd had the mayor call this meeting for today it was with high expectation that the vote might finally run his way.

It must.

Ramont had made a mint from his

high valley operation but his lifelong habit of living far beyond his means meant he required a big influx of profit to keep Ramont Lumber afloat and maintain the lifestyle he'd always enjoyed to the hilt.

Citizens were filing through the meeting-hall doorway upon his arrival. Ramont doffed his hat and smiled. In back of him, his bodyguards kept their hats on and glared warningly at the clerks, cooks, cowhands and landowners crowding the gallery. In Hardesty, Ramont had always gone to great lengths to present a gentlemanly and moderate image to offset the poisonous reputation his methods had earned for him up in the valley. Many now seemed too exhausted to resist any longer the concept of Maxwell Ramont, responsible and concerned businessman and solid citizen. Yet there remained a hard core which mistrusted him violently, hated his guts, and who might not even be above endangering him, hence the escort with guns under their jackets.

His powerful, black-mustached countenance lighted up with genuine pleasure for the first time when he saw the tall, dark-suited woman standing with a group of his most outspoken enemies.

'Lydia, how good of you to come.'

'Hello, Maxwell. I must say you are looking very confident today.'

'And why not, dear lady?' His smile was warm despite the difficulties her opposition had caused him. Sure, he wanted the timber on her farm, but he wanted her even more. He'd thought he was making real progress in that direction before a certain drifter had ridden into the basin. He glanced around and said, 'The great hunter not with us today?'

'No. But I wish he was. I suppose you know the opposition of some towards you is weakening, Maxwell. I suspect that is why you called this meeting, of course.'

'Me? I had nothing to do with it, Lydia.'

'Tell me another.' Her look intrigued him. Ramont considered himself an expert on women but found Lydia Creighton a tough one to read. Her husband had vanished in Canada, probably dead, yet she refused to consider herself a widow woman and held all men, himself included, at arm's length. He often suspected the reason she maintained a kind of friendship with him was more in the interests of keeping an eye upon the enemy rather than anything more personal. But she was worried today, he could tell. And that made him feel even more confident of his prospects as he gallantly guided her inside to help the town decide whether or not the basin was sufficiently demoralized by wolves, winter weather, adversity, empty pockets and capricious acts of God — such as raging bears — to change the vote from anti-logging to pro. The meeting must see him emerge a winner. It must.

He emerged two hours later looking ten years older. He was followed by the mayor acompanied by Lydia Creighton and the day's unexpected and unwelcome guest, Sheriff Henley from Milltown.

Ramont never packed a gun. He paid others to do his dirty work. Even so, if he was toting a shooting iron at this moment — as jubilant anti-loggers flowed out of the hall to gather triumphantly around the tall badgeman — he just might have been tempted to haul it out and give Henley six up against his gold watch chain.

For the lawman had just mounted the podium uninvited to deliver as damning an anti-logging tirade as Ramont could have imagined in his worst nightmare. From that moment on the vote had become a formality. Forget about hard times, the wolf plague and the rest, the lawman had thundered. Timber was still the prime issue in Jubilee Basin, and every man, woman or child who loved this place and didn't wish to see their basin converted into a disaster zone like Ramont Valley, must,

must, must vote against the mayor's proposal to throw it open to the loggers. And they had proceeded to vote that way, almost to a man.

'Hard luck, Ramont. Better luck next time, maybe.'

The newsman was smirking like the cat that ate the cream. Ramont felt like creaming him — with a fist. Lydia smiled and waved as she left, and he gritted his teeth. Never before had he so bitterly regretted a decision he'd taken several months earlier: to get what he wanted down here through bribery, diplomacy and persuasiveness, when what he plainly should have done was employ the same brutal techniques which had got him what he wanted up the valley.

Fear of the formidable sheriff had driven him to take that reluctant path, and now the same man had undermined him again.

This lumberman needed a double shot of red-eye bad.

He was heading for the Chinook

when a look-out sighted a rider coming in across the snowy hills to the south. Ramont paid no attention until one of his bruisers entered the saloon a short time later to announce that someone was looking for him. Someone named Whiskey.

8

Brothers of the Wind

'No mystery,' said the Chief. 'Simple.'

'I had my gun in that big killer's face and didn't shoot . . . and you're sayin' that was simple? How do you figure?'

Burns Wagons gulped down half a wild onion.

'You same, you and wolf. Only want be free and crazy. First day, wolf could kill Long Hair but only warns. Now you could kill him, don't shoot.' He smiled hugely and spread long arms wide. 'Simple. You like brothers — brothers of the wind.'

'And you're loco.'

'Where Long Hair go?'

'To find someone with some brains, I reckon.'

* * *

'What sort of a kiss was that, Chet Beautel?'

'Huh?'

'I've had hotter smooches from my pet goldfish, damnit.'

Beautel grinned. They were taking coffee at the Tinhorn Hash House and Dixie Lee was the best looker in the place — he wasn't sure how smart she was. He leaned towards her to try and do better but she turned her head away. She wanted to sulk.

'You weren't so chilly Saturday night,' she pouted. 'That's if you remember Saturday night?'

Sure he remembered. Saturday night had been memorable — all night long. Dixie was his kind of woman, pretty, friendly and uninhibited. He was good with girls like this mainly due to the fact that they seemed to sense he would treat them right without getting too serious about things. Drifters could never be too serious. And mostly, neither were sweet bouncy girls like Dixie Lee.

'Sorry,' he said. 'I was thinkin' . . . '

'Of her, I suppose?'

'Her?'

'Don't act dumb, Chet Beautel. You know who I mean. The widow woman. Don't try and tell me there's not something going on between you two. You're always stopping by out there, and I've seen the way she looks at you here in town.'

He was startled, genuinely so. 'You're crazy, girl. I'm just helpin' them out. Anyway, she doesn't see me that way. Why should she? She's a lady and I'm just here huntin' wolves.'

'I've seen what I've seen . . . ' Her expression softened. She reached out and squeezed his hand. 'She's sweet on you, handsome, but tell me you don't feel the same about her.'

That was easy for him to do. Lydia Creighton might be one of the finest women he'd ever met, but that was as far as it went. Wanderers didn't get serious about women like that, while sensible women in turn certainly never

176

entertained notions about any man who lived out of his saddle-bags.

No. Dixie was all the way wrong. But he soon cajoled her back into a good mood, walked her home, promised to see her again next time he was in town, then headed for the livery.

Half-way there, Beautel halted to stare out at the mighty tiers of dark forests climbing the basin's walls under a cloudless sky. Times like this he imagined he could feel Deerkiller out there, maybe staring down. The thought caused him to grin and shake his head. Somehow he just didn't seem to be able to work up any real enmity towards that critter, even at times felt a kind of admiration for a critter that was only defending its own patch.

The truth was he was more focused on the wolf packs and considered them the real menace here. And right on cue, it seemed, they began howling far out towards Fastness Range as he strolled on for the stables.

He was going back up there tonight.

He shook his head again as he thought of Dixie suspecting Lydia Creighton might be sweet on him.

Crazy.

He let his fingers run lightly over the indentations of the cart-horse's prints. He rubbed his fingers against his jacket to increase their sensitivity as he now traced the impressions left in the damp earth by the iron-shod wheels of the wagon.

'Toting a fair load,' he murmured, every bit as wary now, hours later, as he'd been when the mixed bear and wolf tracks had led him into the confrontation with Deerkiller.

In that case Beautel had known exactly what he was tracking. Up here, approaching the broad canyon mouth where the glittering wonder of Fortress Mountain filled the sky beyond, he only knew he was dogging a horse and wagon.

Yet this was no place for a wagon trail, and he had still had no notion where the trace was taking him.

All he knew was that the marks were fresh, and that his curiosity wouldn't allow him to quit until he found out who in his right mind would want to drive up here at any time.

The canyon proved wide with several lesser canyons branching off it. A half-mile in, still walking warily with rifle at the ready, he came to a junction where the relatively well-used trail swung off along a western arm of the main canyon. He followed it for some two or three hundred yards more until he glimpsed a section of fence.

Stranger and stranger.

Hugging the wall now, he eased his way through the drifts before halting at a noise. Crystal clear and close by sounded a wolf's short sharp bark. Cocking the rifle and licking dry lips, he moved on slowly. He could still only see the top of the steel wire fence which appeared to stretch from one side of this flanking canyon to the other.

Then he sighted the building.

It resembled a saddlebag bunkhouse

attached to a primitive galley, with thin smoke drifting from a blackened tin chimney. An enclosed and roofed-over dogtrot led from the bunkhouse to a windowless shed, the entire construction abutting the fence.

He took two more wary steps before stopping dead when he realized that the fence and the walls blocking off the canyon formed a two-acre enclosure containing some twenty to thirty young wolves.

He let the hiss of a held breath go as he hunkered down to absorb fully what he was seeing. Already several of the animals were pausing to stare his way, sniffing the air with black nostrils. The wolves appeared healthy and well fed although their manner was wild and aggressive, warning they were not pets of any kind.

Then he glimpsed the wagon parked on the far side, half-obscured by the bunkhouse. It was a sturdy mountain cart fitted out with what appeared to be a wire cage for transporting animals.

There was no sign of life apart from the wolves now staring his way beneath that fluttering gray banner of wood-smoke, sniffing and baring their teeth.

Long minutes passed. Beautel's brain was working at full tilt. The only explanation for what he was seeing sounded crazy, even to him. Yet what else was he to make of this hideaway other than that it was something he'd never dreamed existed anyplace, namely a breeding farm for wolves.

The animals he saw were of varying ages and stages of development, from chubby cubs maybe five or six weeks old, still with their lactating mothers, ranging up to mature bitches and dog wolves practically fully grown with the beginning of stiff adult ruffs beneath their chins.

There were metal water troughs and wooden feeding-bins along the fence, with flaps through which food and water could be added without an attendant being obliged to enter the enclosure. That had to be a chore no man would want to undertake unless equipped with a suit of armour and maybe a Gatling gun.

On the far side was a wired-over pathway leading from the compound to a gate. A loading chute? he pondered. Was this how the wolves were either lured or driven to be loaded onto that cage cart for transportation?

Transportation, Beautel? Just exactly what are you thinking?

That answer was slowly coming clear, despite his initial doubts.

If this were indeed a breeding place for wolves, a well laid-out operation into which considerable money and effort had obviously been put, then it logically followed that there must be a purpose behind it all, a 'market'.

But who would buy wolves? And for what purpose?

It was when he focused on this aspect that his mind first caught hold of the tip-ass end of an answer. Ever since his arrival in the basin, and admittedly with most of his attention focused on

Deerkiller, Beautel had been continually puzzled by the basin's unnaturally high wolf population. The locals seemed to understand Deerkiller's long vendetta completely, but nobody could explain the presence of so many lesser wolves.

He felt almost certain, crouched here in back of a huge, snow-heavy boulder, watching the sleek gray shapes pad to and fro across his field of vision, that what he was seeing was the explanation.

This told him the wolf plague of the basin had not occurred naturally but was deliberately engineered. Men were responsible. But who and why? Who would go to such lengths to inflict misery and terror upon an entire community, and what could they hope to gain?

His thoughts seemed to be leading him somewhere when of a sudden the wolves began to show excitement, leaping high against the fence and rattling it with the weight of their bodies.

Too late, Beautel sensed a presence. Before he could turn, something hard jammed into his kidneys. He whipped his head around to stare up at the huge figure looming over him, a bearded, buffalo-robed apparition clutching a shotgun. The man had come up upon him without one whisper of sound.

'Haircut, you are in a whole mess of trouble,' breathed Torn Whiskey. Then the weapon reversed with blinding speed and the heavy steel-reinforced oak butt smashed against Beautel's temple. The last thing he heard as he pitched into blackness was the excited howling of the wolves.

★　★　★

The light at the far end of the pitch-black tunnel enclosing him appeared first as a speck quickly expanding to a spot which shimmered and danced tantalizingly, threatening to self-extinguish any moment before suddenly erupting into a totally blinding light that assaulted his eyes and sent shooting pains through his skull.

Beautel groaned and rolled over on his belly, clenching his eyes tight shut against the glare. Gradually he grew conscious of the taste of blood in his mouth and felt the bite of rawhide thongs at wrists and ankles.

When eventually he could open his eyes again it was to realize he was indoors surrounded by sacks of provisions, cans of tinned beef and assorted tools and implements of a kind necessary for the maintenance of a farm of some kind.

The farm!

He came jolting back to reality in a rush. His first reaction was that it had to be one hell of a lot better to come conscious indoors, even hurting and trussed up like a thanksgiving turkey, than out there in that damned compound filled with wolves.

He raised his head. No sign of Whiskey. He swallowed painfully twice, then shouted, 'Where are you, scum?

Are you lookin' to fetch yourself twenty years in Northwest Prison for this?'

No response. No human voice, that was. But the wolves heard and they reacted. He could hear them jumping and shaking the fence in their excitement. He knew they could smell him, understood how his presence would inflame them.

How long had he been unconscious?

He studied the shadows on the walls and made a guess. Mid-afternoon, meaning he'd lain here for several hours.

The animals began settling after a time until it was again quiet out there. Chet sat up and began to struggle with his bonds. He eventually succeeded in snapping the tether rope which secured him to a ring-bolt anchored in the floor. Yet the thongs held fast even though he sensed the hint of a weakening in the rawhide, which was old and frayed. He worked until pain and exhaustion called a halt. Forced to lie back and rest, he allowed his thoughts free rein.

Tom Whiskey worked for Ramont.

Ramont wanted to log the basin.

Whiskey was farming wolves, and it was the wolf plague that was driving basin folk to the brink of selling up their land and timber to Ramont — giving him what he wanted and getting out.

Too simple?

Too fanciful, more like it.

Yet the more he thought on it while continuing to struggle with his bonds, the more certain he grew that he was on the right track. He had to be. Nothing else even came close to making any kind of sense.

He suddenly went still, wrists and ankles soaked in blood now, with the thongs tantalizingly looser yet still holding. The first warning alarm rang when the wolves started up snarling and barking; they sounded either angry or hungry, maybe both. Next came the clip clop of hoofs and the creak of wagon axles which were eventually drowned out by Whiskey's harsh shout.

'Bark, you bastards, bark! Come on, who wants a chunk of old Tom? You, you wall-eyed mongrel? Well, come on, come make a try.' The fence shook violently and Beautel heard the sound of something hard striking the wire. A stick or whip handle maybe. 'Devil dog scum! Go for the throat. Attack! Kill, you vermin, kill!'

The racket reached a climax, a violent eruption of animal fury which did not begin to subside until Beautel heard the clomp of bootheels approaching across bare boards outside.

Whiskey was coming.

An involuntary gasp of pain squeezed through the prisoner's locked teeth as he gave the tethers everything he had. More give, but still not enough. He heard Whiskey drag something metallic along the fence, taunting his charges into a final frenzy. Then the door jerked open and the man stood there framed against the snow-light with a blur of crimson jaws showing beyond the huge frame.

'The pretty ones are angry, Haircut,' he panted with relish, setting his whip aside. He lumbered to the single wire-covered window overlooking the pens, raised the glass. The sounds poured in; howling, teeth clashing, a lobophile's nightmare. 'I keep 'em that way so that when they finally get set loose every man is somethin' they hate worse even than you're gunna hate dyin'.'

Beautel felt a chill.

He'd expected this. If he figured right then Whiskey would have reported his capture back to Ramont, who'd have no option but to decide he could not afford to allow him to live. He was hoping Whiskey would not notice the blood. His flesh was afire but he continued to work his wrists behind his back as his captor toyed with his revolver and straddled a protesting chair. The man mountain showed all his tobacco-stained teeth in a grotesque grin.

'Too bad, hot-shot. If you'd stuck to

your knittin' and kept after old Killer and let everythin' else go hang, you'd have been okay. Sure, the boss was pretty sour about you gettin' cozy with his woman. But he wouldn't have rubbed you out just on that score. He's way too smart for that. He's so smart that them rubes down there got no idea howcome they are havin' all this wolf trouble and — '

'Where did Ramont get his idea for all this?' Beautel broke in, discreetly but fiercely straining his ankle bones against the rawhide beneath a chair. He must play for time. 'Wasn't Deerkiller scarin' hell out of the ranchers enough for him without him goin' to these lengths?'

Whiskey's deep chuckle filled the room. The .44 was dwarfed in his hairy wombat of a hand, and he kept dry-snapping the hammer.

'Hell, Haircut, you just set your finger right on it. Ole Killer. When the boss seen how that big varmint's midnight raidin' parties had the rubes

190

runnin' round like headless chickens, and keepin' in mind that Whoremaster Henley was watchin' everythin' he done so close, it suddenly hit him like a bombshell that if one wolf could do all that, what might fifty do . . . a hundred even?'

'You're sayin' he started this some time back, then?' Sweat was breaking out over Beautel's face from his exertions. He marvelled that the other still didn't seem to notice. 'How long?'

'Hey, I'm sharp to you, boy. You're cadgin' extra minutes to live, ain't you?' The muzzle of the gun stabbed at Beautel. 'Well, cain't rightly blame you, I guess. O' course you know it's only on account you're a dead man already that I can level with you, don't you?'

He chuckled. His belly jiggled. He was enjoying this.

'It was about a year ago Max hit on his big idea. He knew I'd hunted wolves on and off all my life, and he knew I'd jump at the chance to make some real money. Even then he was thinkin' ahead to the time when the high valley would be all logged out, and decided if one wolf could scare the bastards a hundred could do a hundred times better and faster job. So that gave me plenty of time to trap and rear up enough wolves to get started, while he had his boys put this place together up here where even God wouldn't find it. Soon I had the whole thing runnin' like clockwork so that by the start of winter I was ready to load up my first consignment, run 'em down almost to Hardesty one black night, and before daylight they was off killin' cows. Some great plan, huh?'

'Only it didn't work. You've brought good people to their knees but they are still holdin' out. Ramont's big plan's a failure. Just like you, you poor miserable loser.'

He wanted to draw the man to him. He succeeded. As Whiskey lunged, upsetting his chair in his haste to get at him, Beautel brought up his partially freed feet and drove a brutal double kick into the groin, heels sinking deep in spongy flesh.

Tom Whiskey was spewing as he jackknifed. Beautel erupted from the floor, almost gagging from the murderous pain in his arms as he threw everything into one final desperate surge of power against the bonds.

His tortured hands burst loose as Whiskey was unbending from the jackknife. The man's face was ashen and murderous as their eyes locked at a range of inches. Beautel sensed the knee whipping in and pivoted to catch it on the hip. Stumbling, with rawhide still encumbering his legs, he managed to piston a smashing elbow into the bearded jaw. He followed it up with a knee to the guts his adversary was not agile enough to dodge.

The huge frame sagged and a sickening exhalation of stinking breath hit Beautel squarely in the face. He ignored it. The power was coursing through him. Lightning-fast, he seized two handfuls of shirt to hoist the limp bull almost off its feet, then charged the window. The human battering-ram smashed the glass and bowed the reinforcing wire backing.

The wolf yard went loco.

Whiskey was screaming as a grim Beautel hauled him back off the window, then dug his heels in and charged the wire again, holding his floundering burden before him.

There was a vicious twanging sound as the wire mesh gave way. Whiskey was caught up half-way through the window, half-way into the enclosure.

'Oh no! For pity's sake!' he howled, sounding more like a sick girl than 300 pounds of evil.

The howl became a scream of agony as the first set of fangs bit through buffalo robe and several layers of clothing to find the flesh beneath.

It was a tight squeeze to get that vast carcass all the way through the smashed window. But Beautel would not be denied. A final surging thrust of power, and a screaming Tom Whiskey was crashing backwards into the yard where a ferocious gray tide instantly engulfed him.

Chet reeled back from the window, dizzy from exertion, staggering from pain and loss of blood. He dropped onto a chair to fumble with his ankle bonds, was ripping the last one away when a terrific slam against the window brought his head jerking up. He was staring at the head and shoulders of a wolf slowly sliding back out of sight.

His jaw sagged as he staggered upright.

He'd conceived his window plan and put it into operation all in the same desperate split second. No time to consider consequences. An obvious one was that if a man could go through the window in one direction, a wolf could come through in the other.

He was looking round wildly for something to block the opening with, when the leaping wolf came flying right on through, crashing into a pile of implements but nimbly regaining its feet.

Beautel dived for Whiskey's dropped gun.

The wolf was almost on him as he began firing. The savage head exploded in a grisly spray of blood, gray matter and smoke. Beautel hurled the carcass off him and staggered outside like a drunk.

He looked back once, winced. They'd dragged Whiskey thirty yards clear of the bunkhouse. He was still moving feebly although ripped and torn from head to toe. Closer, big gray shapes were leaping at the bunkhouse wall, bounding from a barrel and using it as a stepping-stone to propel them up to the window.

There was nothing like sheer desperation to clear a dazed man's senses and get the adrenaline rushing.

He was made of iron. He felt no pain. He ran like a deer and made it to the horse and wagon in one headlong rush, hurled himself into the seat and whipped the reins free of the whip socket.

'Heeyahh!' he roared, laying on the leather. The wild-eyed quarter horse lunged into the harness and they were off, scattering snow and one half-grown wolf from their path as they executed a tight half-circle turn on two wheels, rocked level, then followed the course of the box canyon at a gallop for the steep downhill trail.

He kept triggering back to leave more gray forms writhing and jetting great gouts of blood into the snow, until the gun ran empty.

He flung it aside and concentrated simply on driving and staying alive as they went roaring down-hill like an avalanche.

9

Staying Alive

Nobody was paying any attention to a crazy old Dakota seated cross-legged in the middle of the street in the deepening dusk. Hardesty was accustomed to the strange and often outlandish habits of Chief Burns Wagons. Some day, so citizens often predicted, enough folks would get together to push a motion through Council to the effect that the old red reprobate be given his marching orders and dispatched either to Skyline Plateau or the nearest reservation.

Apart from irreverence, a total disrespect for authority and his bitter opposition to the wild-horse trade here, the same critics also considered it untenable that Hardesty should harbor a savage, even an ancient one, known to have committed atrocities against the Bluecoats back in the days when this region was still part of the Red Empire.

'He should be shot, not tolerated,' the mayor had publicly proclaimed on one occasion when Burns Wagons's direct intervention had prevented Buckner's team of horse-hunters capturing a bunch of wild mustangs up on Elk Mesa. Many tended to agree. Yet the prospect of actually doing something about the dangerous old warrior generally seemed more daunting than the trouble. In any event, the town had been too preoccupied with other far more serious matters about which to worry itself during this grim winter.

So the Chief sat all alone in the rutted street tonight, hands dangling over bony knees, his stare focused on a patch of dirty snow while his lips chanted an ancient shaman's prayer which had to do with war.

None of the passers-by seemed to notice that the Chief wore a heavy gold chest-medallion, and likely would not have made anything of it even if they had.

He'd worn the medallion as a young and limber buck, howling at the north-country moon as army wagons were engulfed in soaring tongues of flame. The Chief had donned his sacred talisman at sundown today when the mayor's men reached town with yet another batch of half-starved mustangs to swell the mob already imprisoned in the over-crowded Double Forty corral in back of Buckner's Store.

The old Dakota was communicating with his gods for guidance as he had in the glory days when he'd burned the wagons. As he chanted, grunted, swayed and took a little whiskey against the cold, it seemed clear to him that the spirits favored direct action against the horse-hunters.

'Chief!'

The voice tried to penetrate his cocoon of concentration. It succeeded. He looked up, glaring. The glare vanished. Lydia Creighton was one of his friends in the basin. He didn't have many. In truth he'd only struck one other he might rate that high, yet now Long Hair seemed to have vanished.

Direct and clear-speaking as always, the woman informed him that she was enquiring after Beautel. Did the Chief know anything of his whereabouts?

He shook his head.

'Maybe Deerkiller get him,' he grunted morosely. Then he added contritely: 'But then, maybe not,' and promptly returned to his rocking and chanting.

Next, Lydia tried the Chinook before going on to Beautel's hotel. Beautel wasn't there. She was speaking with the hotel desk clerk when Ramont entered the lobby at the head of a large bunch of men from the valley.

Before the lumber king sighted her, Lydia noted instantly that he appeared to be in a violent mood. But when Ramont caught her eye he instantly blanked his expression and crossed briskly to the desk.

'Lydia, I thought you were returning to the spread.'

'I was, but I grew concerned about Chet. He's been gone twenty hours, Maxwell. Have you heard anything of him?'

'Not a word.' He smiled reassuringly. 'But I would not concern myself, my dear. After all, that's his natural habitat out there, isn't it? The wild man in the wilds?'

'It's not amusing,' she retorted, and hurried off to resume her search, leaving Ramont leaning one greatcoated elbow on the desk and massaging his jaw thoughtfully.

His men gathered round. This bunch represented his tough inner circle of protectors and enforcers. The Ramont Valley muscle. All were rugged up in trail gear, having only just arrived from the valley in response to the boss man's summons.

Ramont was having a testing time in the wake of the sheriff's undermining of his meeting, followed by Whiskey's late afternoon visit here from the 'farm'. By this time he expected to have received word from Whiskey that Beautel was dead. He checked his watch, then crooked a finger at Darcy.

'Take three men and get up to the farm and find out what the hell is going on,' he snapped. The four left immediately and Ramont eyed the others with one eyebrow jammed down hard and the other cocked high. This was his thinking look. 'One way or another I'm going to turn this council decision around,' he announced finally. 'These hold-out sons of bitches are going to sign their leases over to me one freaking way or another . . . '

He broke off at an uneasy thought. So much on his mind today, he was tending to overlook details.

'That damned lawdog did leave, didn't he?'

A husky jack nodded and Ramont relaxed. But only a little. Soon he began to speak again, thinking out loud. There was a feeling in him today that everything was suddenly in the melting-pot, that victory was there for the taking but only if he played his cards right. Thoughtful and intent, he started in pitching a plan of action on how he might still carry the day in Hardesty without running foul of the law, for Sheriff Henley of Milltown was still the only man in the region he truly feared.

Yet his listeners kept shaking their heads. The boss man's plans were over-hasty and only half thought through, and it showed. Ramont's face flushed with anger, yet he knew they were right to blow cold. He was best when he had time to scheme and plot at his leisure, not under pressure the way he was at that moment.

He cursed and was lighting another stogie when the hotel's double doors swung inwards to admit a gust of snow and someone whom he was never pleased to see, and especially not at this moment, came striding in.

'Throw him out!' he barked.

The Chief stopped when he saw the

lumbermen moving in on him. He shrugged in what seemed an accepting way, then his right arm blurred and he came up with a foot-long knife once used for skinning buffalo.

'Peace!' he said, looking as peaceable as a stick-poked polecat. The hardcases immediately backed up and glanced at Ramont for direction. Then the Indian added almost benignly, 'You do Chief good turn. Until he sees you he does not know if he should do what spirits say he must. But I see you and I know that buzzard walks with dove. Buzzard mayor traps the wonderful ones and buzzard timberman buy them. Buzzards both. And seeing buzzard, Chief's thoughts grow clear as mountain lake.'

He turned and left, still lithe and graceful despite gray hair and wrinkles that cut as deep as canyons.

But crazy, of course.

'I shouldn't let that moth-eaten old sonuva rile me, but he does,' Ramont complained. 'Now where was I . . . '

It took him some moments to recover

concentration following the interruption. Yet no such confusion troubled Burns Wagons now as he made his long-legged way down an alley towards the corrals.

His mind was crystal-clear at last.

It was true what he'd said at the hotel. He knew what he wanted to achieve yet felt he'd needed some sign or omen to convert him from mere protester to activist. Meeting the timber boss reminded him how deeply he hated every rich white man in Hondo County: Ramont for sure, but the mayor even worse.

Mayor Buckner — the mustangs' enemy.

They began to whicker in the freezing gloom at his approach; mares, wild-eyed colts, the proud stallions, all the foals and those old ones imprisoned for the first time in their long free lives.

Apart from the bunch run in just that day, every broomtail in the big corral knew the Chief. He was the friend who visited them every day to bring them treats and to talk to them and stroke trembling muzzles. They would bite another man's hand off at the wrist but he could do what he liked with them because they trusted him.

But when they were sold they would be whipped, broken, enslaved or butchered for horsemeat. This would make the mayor even richer, all his evil horse-hunters would be well paid, and Hardesty would celebrate the evil event.

His gangling shape moved along the fence, seeing like a cat in the gloom. The animals filled his senses. Skinny-legged, lion-hearted, wonderful mustangs every one, they were descendants of the ancient Barb breed which had once carried Burns Wagons and his warrior ancestors to glorious victories, now caged and humiliated but still fierce and proud.

Like him.

Here was the long-jawed roan which had crippled a Buckner wrangler during its capture, there that sway-backed, long-legged palomino the Chief called Golden. Indian Jug, Big Feet, Red

Chief and Dakota. They were here tonight and all were restless and whistling softly as though realizing something was blowing in the wind, something wild and exciting. And yet they could not believe it when the big heavy gate swung wide and the man was standing there before them, beckoning them to join him, the gold medallion on his bony chest winking in the night.

When Burns Wagons stepped to one side the wild mustangs flooded out like a roaring torrent to storm the length of the main street through the town on their unstoppable flight for the high country.

★   ★   ★

Riders on the trail below!

The instant he glimpsed the dark silhouettes against the white backdrop, Beautel knew it had to be trouble. He was still too high and remote up here to expect any chance encounters. Ramont

Valley riders was his first and only guess.

Reining the horse back a notch, he glanced over his shoulder. The trail was a dark ribbon against the pearl-white earth, flanked by dark stands of trees where it climbed over a series of terraces all the way up to the wolf canyon. Tiny moving dots were visible higher up. He doubted the wolves were pursuing him. Most likely they were running simply because they were now free. But he also knew they were very hungry.

It made good sense for him to keep on for the bottom lands just as fast as he could make it. But what of these riders climbing towards him?

Where the trail dipped sharply he hauled the rig back to a trot and leapt to the ground. The horse continued on, the cage wagon swaying from side to side as it climbed out of the depression. By this, Beautel was trotting along through the trees with Tom Whiskey's rifle in his hands and his sixshooter thrusting upwards from his belt, keeping parallel to the trail.

The riders began yelling the moment the slowing rig was sighted up ahead. They quickly drew abreast and dragged the outfit to a halt.

'What the hell is this? This is Whiskey's rig, but where is he? Hey, Tom! You there?'

' 'Course he ain't there. Anyone can see that. Somethin's happened to the fat bastard.'

'I reckon there's no point in us climbin' any higher, do you?' a bearded heavyweight said nervously. 'I mean, if Whiskey's run into trouble of some kind, would Ramont want us to keep right on ridin' and mebbe get ourselves shot up?'

'Damn right he would,' barked the tall rider in a weather-stained mackinaw who seemed to be in charge.

Invisible in the trees, Beautel waited, patient as a hostile. Ramont's toughs sounded edgy. Even so, he was expecting they'd decide to keep on. If they did, he might get to reclaim the wagon and resume his journey.

He sensed the wolf before seeing it. It was gaunt and dark-bodied with fangs that glinted whitely in the gloom in the instant it launched itself at him from behind. He hurled his body aside, not knowing whether it might be a Whiskey wolf which had trailed him. There was no time to think. Somehow he managed to get the rifle barrel between himself and the feral shape as it twisted to come back at him. He triggered. The wolf's body leapt high in a huge convulsive backflip.

Before it struck ground, Beautel was rolling away and blasting toward the trail.

The first gun-toting rider rode directly into a bullet and was tumbling back over his horse's rump as, lightning-fast, Beautel again changed positions to trade shots with a beanpole on a buckskin which was rearing away from the man's rolling corpse.

The beanpole buckled in the middle.

Beautel got behind a larch and began firing from the hip, sweeping the trailside with a scything volley.

They were the first white men he'd ever killed. But he'd fought it out with Indians often enough in the Rocky Mountains to remain cool and deadly when the chips were down.

There were four men down and two fleeing downslope by the time it was over. Immediately Beautel quit cover and raced swiftly downslope in pursuit of Tom Whiskey's rattling wagon.

★ ★ ★

Cosgrove was first man to sell out to the enemy.

The grizzled graybeard was one of the original pioneers of Jubilee Basin, a leathery old sourdough of a dirt farmer with two grown sons employed by the mayor in his horse-hunting enterprise.

The Cosgroves had been hanging on by the skin of their teeth waiting for Buckner to sell his ever-increasing horse herd in order that the sons might be paid, thus providing enough to see them through to high summer.

The stampede had dashed that hope. There would be no sale, no payday, and old man Cosgrove, who'd always applauded the sheriff's efforts to keep the basin logger-free, had at last had enough.

A surprised and gratified Max Ramont now owned full logging rights to all timber found upon the Cosgroves' Tiptoe ranch.

The floodgates had opened.

The mayor was seated alongside the big desk in his wide-open store, now commanded by a beaming Ramont and his agents. He sat tugging at his goatee trying to figure if his massive loss with the mustangs would in time be compensated for by his involvement with Ramont on the logging and the boom it would surely bring here in the basin.

The store gallery, usually dark and deserted at nine at night in winter, was crowded with people from town and country, debating, wrangling, agitated and bitter. In one way or another most had been relying upon the always highly profitable mustang sale to keep them going. A number of men were employed as horse-hunters for Buckner here, while provisioners and suppliers were always waiting for Buckner to get cashed up and settle his accounts with them. The enterprise managed to keep the wheels turning in this wolf-plagued community. Now everything was gone with the disappearance of that last twitching mustang tail out across the north slopes, and Hardesty had at long last had enough.

In just one twenty-four hour period they had suffered despair, been brought back from the brink by the lawman's support, now were in the pits again in the aftermath of this disaster which few believed had been accidental.

On a cold spring night which felt more like the dead heart of winter, weary men, disheartened women and even children were asking one another the same bleak question:

Why fight any longer?

'Friends, this is not a defeat but a triumph,' assured Ramont as yet another beaten 'stayput' sheep rancher shuffled forward, ready to sign anything put in front of him. Ramont wondered why he had not foreseen the potential benefit in turning the wild horses loose himself.

As if somehow sensing that the town was suffering some sort of bitter defeat, the wild wolves were out there howling, triumphantly, so it seemed. And maybe Deerkiller was with them, relishing the victory.

But the wolves' triumph wouldn't last. In due course, exposed to axe, snigging lines and sawmill, along with the timbermen's total disregard for the future health and fertility of the basin, Jubilee would become a desolate wasteland just like Ramont Valley and it would be no place for either good people or wolves.

The reality was that there was but

one real winner here tonight. And while the line of landholders continued shuffling into the store to surrender in return for a bank check with Ramont's signature on it, those still struggling to find some reason to justify holding out peered miserably through the windows at that winner basking in his triumph.

None was more bitter or worried than Lydia Creighton tonight.

She realized that she also would be forced to give in now the ravagers were coming in anyway. Yet she was even more concerned about Chet Beautel, the long-haired 'wild man' from the mountains, whom she had not realized was growing important to her until he went missing.

Observing it all from the distance of his lamplit office across the way, newsman Nathan Pooley sat with his pipe between his teeth and pen in hand, chronicling the last free day of the basin he loved for future generations.

Burns Wagons was first to hear the horses as he was farthest from the noises of Main Street, as far out as the Pioneer River bridge in truth. Thus far they didn't know who'd released the animals, but the Chief sensed that some, such as the mayor, might have some pretty strong suspicions. The Chief might well be ecstatic with his triumph and the chaos it brought in its wake, but he was not suicidal. White folks tended to make snap judgments on perceived Indian crimes, then act upon them, so he chose to stay well clear until the dust settled.

He ducked for cover as hard hoofs hammered across the bridge. Minutes later, the general store's doors were shut tight with the would-be sellers instructed to return the following day. It seemed only the logger faction knew what was happening, and they were not saying as Ramont bawled orders that sent his men scattering throughout the town to take up positions on the outskirts.

It was when they realized that the timbermen were toting guns in their hands as they hurried about their mysterious business that the prudent citizens of Hardesty wisely retreated to their homes.

Yet another disaster on its way? they asked one another in grim resignation. You could bet on it. The place they loved seemed to have become that kind of town.

10

Those Who Lived

Beautel was whipping the cart horse along the rutted trace of the final stretch of straight trail leading to town, ducking his head beneath the low-hanging limbs of the great sentinel pines when the apparition seemed to rise out of the snow before him.

His left hand took over both reins and his right filled with sixgun. Still stretched taut as rawhide following the brutal shootout higher up, he was ready to fill more graves on what was surely a night of blood if that was what it took to get where he was going.

He stayed his trigger-finger, kicked on the brake and jerked back violently on the ribbons as he identified the long gaunt figure and sorrel features of the ghostly figure holding both arms above its head.

The lathered wagon horse blew foam from flared nostrils as it ploughed to a stop bare inches from the Chief, who did not move one inch.

'Hau,' he grunted, just as though they'd met on Main Street at midday.

'How, goddamnit!' Then: 'What the hell are you doin' here, old man?'

Burns Wagons moved round the blowing horse to stand by the front wheel.

'They wait for you like wolves,' he grunted when he could make himself heard above the horse's stertorous blowing. He gestured towards the distant lights. 'Ramont men circle town with weapons. They speak your name with anger.'

'You sure about this?' Beautel panted. He wanted Burns Wagons to be wrong about the danger. He was fit enough to fight all night but didn't want to, not after the slaughter on the trail. But he sensed the shooting wasn't yet done when the phlegmatic Dakota gave an affirmative nod.

'No doubt. Toad-droppings lie in wait for Long Hair in dark.' He made a vicious sideways cutting motion. 'We leave them for wolves to fight over their guts and worms feast on eyeballs. Hau!'

Chet climbed down off the rig unhurriedly and tugged out his tobacco sack. His palms were damp. He was deliberately slowing himself down and throttling back, knowing the old man spoke truly, readying himself to swallow gunsmoke again.

By the time he had his smoke going his pulsebeat had slowed way down and his brain felt cool and clear.

He realized now he should have expected to find trouble waiting here.

Whiskey had tried to kill him, plainly on Ramont's orders. He'd then been forced into a bloody gundown with the logger party he'd encountered along the canyon trail, at the end of which the survivors had galloped off for the town, plainly to alert their master.

Naturally Ramont was lying in wait for him.

But Chet Beautel had the choice between running and fighting again, didn't he?

The grimace that twisted his features as he sucked the last deep draw out of the hand-rolled durham was bitter.

The hell he did!

'You in or out, old man?' he growled roughly, hitching at his gun belt.

Burns Wagons looked offended. 'Chief lead, white-eyes follow.'

Chet grinned broadly as the old man brushed him aside and raised a moccasined foot to a front wheel hub. The unnatural quiet and darkness of the town below was noticeable now, and he reckoned it could prove as bad as Burns Wagons said. But he was not alone. One man you could rely on in a fight was better than a dozen of the suspect kind.

He spat out his cigarette and grabbed for the gunnel rails as the Chief untied the reins and raised them above the horse's glistening rump.

'What the hell are you doin'?' he yelled as he clambered up onto the driver's bench.

'They wait for Whiskey's wagon. So, they will see it.'

'What?'

A slap of the lines sent the horse lurching forward.

'In days when we burn wagons, we call it diversion,' came the shouted response. 'When badmen see wagon they will shoot and chase it. That is when Long Hair will jump and follow aspen line to river and cross fording into town to attack from behind.'

'But . . .'

His words were swallowed by the smash of wheels on frozen earth. He was forced to hang on tight as the horse was lashed into full gallop to go roaring downslope over several hundred yards before suddenly swinging west to jolt violently across the snowfields on a line parallel to the river.

'You'll get us killed!' Beautel protested. But he didn't mean it. The old warrior knew what he was doing. He was an inspiration . . . and Chet only wished he'd had time to ask after Lydia and the boy.

He must believe they had to be safe. For what was waiting him in the town couldn't be averted now.

He was ready to fight again.

The rifles began bellowing from the fringe of town as hidden gunmen identified the late Tom Whiskey's evil-smelling rig jouncing towards them across the snow — while a fleet-footed Beautel legged it away unseen through the woods to pick up the long line of aspen flanking the river which cut Hardesty in half. He covered a half-mile at a loping run, by which time he could glimpse Burns Wagons circling on the far side of town beyond the Halligan wind pump, shooting into the sky and drawing virtually all the hostile fire.

He crossed at the knee-deep fording and went searching for his first gunman.

The gunflashes had given the ambushers' positions away and he'd memorized them all. He knew exactly where to look when he reached the shadowed rear of the feed-and grain-barn. He was able to take the first one out with his gunbutt, but didn't see the other in an alcove across the street until the dark figure jerked up from deep shadow, with light glinting off blued gun steel. Gunblasts chewed big orange holes in the riverside gloom and the battle of Hardesty had begun.

★　★　★

A full score of citizens were huddled inside the church, mostly out-of-towners caught with noplace else to hide when the shooting erupted a half hour earlier. Nobody seemed to know how the battle on the streets was progressing early on but there were reports of several dead already. Nothing on Beautel as yet.

But when the gutsy newsman came

to calm the frightened citizens a short time later he brought good news. He'd just sighted Burns Wagons tearing down a back street in Tom Whiskey's wagon, blasting at a Ramont thug with a shotgun and howling like — well — an Indian on the warpath. Better still, he'd just seen gun-toting towners, inspired by Long Hair and the Chief, emerging from hiding and switching roles from hares to hounds.

The wolves had not settled and their chilling howls provided the eerie back-drop to the battle as gunshots rocked false-fronts and desperate men rushed wildly through smoke-filled streets, shouting and shooting at shadows.

The wolves sounded gleeful as though somehow sensing their two-legged enemies were falling upon one another and might continue to do so until all were gone.

At least that was the theory a sweating Nathan Pooley advanced, but nobody seemed to listen. Crouching behind pews, some praying but many cursing, and all twitching at each new outbreak of gunfire, the citizens of Hardesty were living in fear of the first uplift in the racket that might indicate the trouble was drawing closer.

Everyone yelled when the doors crashed inward and a wild eyed Ramont, bleeding from a shoulder wound and limping heavily, came rushing in with Darcy at his side.

'There she is!' the lumberman shouted, jabbing a finger at Lydia where she sat in a pew cuddling her son. 'Get her, you idiot!'

Louis screamed as Darcy came rushing down the aisle towards them.

'Come on, bitch!' the big man snarled, seizing Lydia by the arm and hauling her bodily from the seat. 'If that dirty Long Hair's gonna get us he'll have to kill you first!'

'Chet?' Lydia gasped as she was dragged for the doors. 'Is he still alive?'

'Alive but not alone!' boomed a familiar voice as a window shattered and the head and shoulders of a towering figure clutching a shotgun appeared like a vision materializing out of the darkness. Burns Wagons jerked trigger to blast a huge hole in the ceiling. 'Bluecoats freeze!'

Maybe in his mind the Chief was still fighting a long-ago battle against another enemy. But his gun eye and trigger finger were as sharp and deadly as they'd ever been in his terror days, and the instant a desperate Ramont jerked up his Colt .45 and touched a shot at him, the shotgun spewed a second time to chop him down.

Ramont went reeling as Beautel came shouldering through the doors in a breakneck rush, lank hair flying as he cannoned off the baptismal font and launched himself into a tremendous headlong dive. He hit Darcy a split second before the man could jerk trigger, smashing him back into a wall with sickening force. Beautel delivered a savage kick to the head and whirled in the same motion to see a bloodied Ramont rising from the floor.

The big man was leaking blood and weeping. Beautel had winged him earlier in a clash at the Chinook saloon where he and the Chief had formed a lethal ambush party of two that drove the loggers to flight with heavy losses when the towner guns chimed in.

He'd tagged Ramont to the church, unaware of his plans to take Lydia hostage.

Despite his pain, Ramont was still struggling to use his gun. Next instant Nathan Pooley came upon him from behind and knocked him senseless with a broken chair leg, the most welcome sight Beautel had seen all day.

Correction. Second most welcome.

Lydia and Louis rushed into his arms and he held them tight. This was his reward, the only one he wanted. He knew already that when the gunsmoke had settled he would be riding on, but suddenly didn't know how the hell he was going to do that without hurting two people who'd already taken too much.

'Come and get it!'

Nobody needed to be called twice, for the aroma of hot biscuits had awakened everyone in the house an hour earlier, but they had been barred from the kitchen by the cook until breakfast was ready to hit the table.

The man in command of the range could cook like a French chef but somehow didn't look the part. Maybe it was the shoulder-length hair, the bandaged forearm and the cigar jutting from one corner of his mouth that made him appear out of place in such a domestic setting. Or more likely it was because all present bar the sheriff had seen Beautel and the Chief take on the timbermen in a bloody battle that had left five men dead, and so still looked more like a deadly hunter than a cook to their eyes.

'Can I help, Chet?'

Lydia Creighton looked somehow younger today, and the Chief didn't miss the way she glanced at Beautel as he shook his head then cleared his throat to speak.

'Everybody set,' he ordered. 'That includes lawmen.'

The toughest peace officer in Hondo County actually grinned, even though his wife swore he'd not done so since their wedding day.

But Henley had good reason to be genial today. Certainly he would have preferred a peaceful solution to the basin's long-running troubles, but was happy to accept resolution by whichever means it came. The lawman believed he had sufficient evidence to get Ramont the rope; he'd had difficulty believing the evidence of his own eyes when he travelled up to the 'wolf farm' actually to see for himself the extraordinary lengths Ramont had gone to in his attempts to drive the landowners out of the basin.

A Ramont henchman had confirmed the information Whiskey had given Beautel on how Ramont had conceived his scheme to pollute the basin with wolves to help drive out the hold-outs. Tom Whiskey had been the ideal man to run his breeding program, but it had cost him his life. Henley had since ordered the remaining wolves destroyed and was confident those at large would be quickly dealt with or run off.

The wolf farm had cost Ramont plenty. But an examination of the logger's books revealed him as a very rich man at the time of his fall. He'd never really needed to log down in the basin. Sheer greed had been the man's undoing.

Everyone laughed when Henley found himself seated alongside the Chief. The law-bringer — and the wild man who recognized no law but his own. Yet as the leisurely meal progressed and conversation flowed freely, the two men talked easily, even amiably, each recognizing that the other had desired the same thing all along, namely peace in the basin. For Henley, that meant no lawbreakers; for Burns Wagons, freed horses running the ranges again.

The guests had already learned of Mayor Buckner's imprisonment on charges of aiding and abetting Ramont, who had already preceded him to the hospital at the county prison. Everyone chatted, drank coffee, did justice to the cooking and the atmosphere was about as relaxed as it could be, considering the circumstances.

But for some reason the cook didn't have an appetite, or have much to say for that matter. And while Henley chatted to Lydia, and Burns Wagons and Pooley, who each found jawboning as natural as breathing, wound one another up, he discreetly headed for the door.

This was a new day and a new start for everyone, he mused. Especially Chet Beautel.

Fresh snow had fallen overnight and the world was pure and clean again. He glanced back at the house as he made for the stables. The basin was coming alive once more and he planned to help the Creightons get their place up and running before moving on.

Moving on.

Sounded right, so he told himself. But why was he uneasy? He halted and drew on his smoke. He knew why. She liked him and so did the kid. He'd helped them out but they needed a hell of a lot more help. But if he stayed longer . . . He shook his head. Maybe he was imagining she'd come to depend on him, that the handsome widow woman might be seeing him as more than just a hand about the place — like Dixie Lee had hinted once.

She was all class. Louis was a fine boy. But he'd found freedom that day in the beaver pond and knew he had to have it every day of the rest of his life.

He shook his head and strolled on.

Fortress Mountain glittered in the early sunshine, and just looking at it rekindled the restlessness in him. Leaning on the corral railing with his cigarette between his teeth, his quiet gray eyes played over the run-down spread.

There was a mess of work to be done hereabouts with no regular man about the place in four years. And Ramont's wolves were still out there; he could see one now standing watching from beneath an elm.

And then there was Deerkiller.

His jaw sagged. Maybe he could overlook the fact that the Creightons needed him around, but what about that big black wolf? That job was still his, he couldn't deny. He'd taken it on; he must finish it.

He ground his teeth. Another tie dragging at him, trying to tempt him to delay? Stay? Maybe get trapped again?

Lydia called from the porch window and it was as he turned that Beautel saw the tracks in the snow. Two sets, they came out of the timber to the south by Paiute Creek to turn sharply south-west on a direct line that led across the Creighton's west pasture, where they had suddenly veered into the very house-yard itself, passing less than ten feet from the window of the supply room where he'd spent the night.

Two sets. The dainty prints of a female and the unmistakable steel-toed prints of a huge timber wolf.

Beautel felt his heart pick up its beat. Sometime during the night Deerkiller had come from God alone knew where to within mere inches of him as he slept.

Why?

The tracks had been left sometime since the early-hours' snowfall. Following the sign with his piercing gaze as they cut away due south from the spread, Beautel realized he could still see them for almost a mile. The tracks did not deviate. The wolves were making for the Fastness region, the remote and lovely high country far from the realm of man, the same place where wolvers had slain the killer's bride and pups many years earlier, but so far as was known, he had never gone back there since.

Beautel had visited the Fastness. There'd been no wolf spoor up there, recent or ancient. But now Deerkiller and his new bride were heading there — after first making sure he knew it.

What was this? A challenge?

Then he remembered what Burns Wagons had said about them — Beautel and the wolf. They were the same; the old Dakota had been emphatic. During the course of his half-hearted hunting he'd felt they were like equals rather than enemies, that, crazily, neither really wanted the other dead — maybe because both were so much alike.

He felt his scalp pull tight. Of course he had no way of being certain of this, he realized, yet he simply knew the great wolf would not be back. Deerkiller had changed. The presence of the female with him told the man so. The wolf war was finally over and men and beasts were longing for peace. The certitude of this was overwhelming, undeniable. They wouldn't meet again in this life but memories were as long as life anyway.

He frowned now as he heard a distant howl. He raised his eyes to the skyline and saw the great wolf standing motionless Their eyes met and locked and then with a flick of the tail and toss of head it was gone.

Deerkiller was free and was telling the man he too was free now. But Beautel knew he was not. Something in the way circumstances had evolved here on the spread was holding him, some kind of loyalty or responsibility that a wandering man really could not afford. But the inside man was surveying the distances and hearing the call of the unknown.

'Chet.'

He turned a little reluctantly. 'Yeah, Lydia?'

She gave him that special smile.

Beautel walked slowly for the house.

★　★　★

'Why not go? Horses free now. Chief ride to California, maybe Mexico. Long Hair come?'

Chet squinted up at the beanpole on horseback.

'You're loco,' he replied. 'You're a thousand years old, and they're used to you here. Well, almost. You could help me lick this spread into shape.'

'Not for long.'

'What?'

Burns Wagons' expression was unreadable.

'Long Hair go too, maybe soon, maybe later. But he go.' He made one of his emphatic gestures. 'Mustangs run, Long Hair run. In blood.'

Beautel stepped back with a scowl. 'You know the set-up out there. They need me. And I need them. You think I want to wind up like you?'

'You same as Chief whether like it or not.' Burns Wagons seemed to enjoy saying this as he turned his gaunt-ribbed appaloosa towards the setting sun. 'Hau!'

Abruptly, he was gone. Beautel yelled after him but he didn't look back. Disgust high in his throat Beautel headed for the livery, changed his mind half-way and turned instead for the saloon, where he drank three quiet beers before deciding it was now time to head back to the place he was reluctantly learning to call home.

He led his mount from the livery as the last of the light left the sky and he stood tall and uncertain, adrift in a strange phase of shifting time while all about him the town he'd helped save lay murmuring in the dusk like a living thing, as though one thousand people beat with a single pulse. But not one thousand and one. Like Burns Wagons, he yearned to be gone, yet felt somehow obligated to remain.

Was he snared again?

He thought on that on the trail out, was still considering it when he reached the lamplit house and saw the horse tied up at the hitch rail by the door.

A horse he didn't know.

Covering the last stretch at the lope, he was swinging down by the live oak tree when the boy came rushing out, yelling unintelligibly, excited, emotional. Beautel started for the house then stopped as Lydia appeared beneath the porch light wearing an expression he couldn't read. She was followed by a man he'd never seen before, yet who seemed strangely familiar.

The fellow was around forty, lean and stooped with dark hair and mustache.

He realized with a jolt it was the man from the photograph on the mantel in the front room.

'Chet,' the woman said, touching the man's arm. 'This is my husband, Phillip. He . . . he's been a prisoner of the Indians. Phillip, this is our kind friend, Mr Beautel.'

Beautel looked sober but his heart sang.

★ ★ ★

The spring day was bitter cold and there were ice-teeth in the sleet that blew down in ragged, boisterous gusts off the giant bluff the Dakotans called Old Grumbler. No game or birds stirred this early, no sign of life stirred in the whole shivering landscape but for the horse slogging its way through the deep drifts of a brokenback ridge and the smiling man in the saddle.

Heading west.

But what was there to smile about on such a day?

Plenty, Beautel knew. Knew it as keenly as he'd ever known anything.

He'd turned his back on a chance to earn 500 bucks, missed out on a fine woman now back in the arms of a man who'd been a captive slave of the Blackfeet in Canada for five long years — the man she was married to.

Now he rode with Hondo County a hundred miles behind, funds were low, the future uncertain and the weather was threatening to turn vicious again.

Yet he rode calm and easy in his

mind. Jubilee Basin had been a test for his decision to return to the old way of life — for the rest of his life. He'd had to hunt a killer wolf, got to know a fine woman and her boy and made a true friend of a crazy old Dakota in order to affirm the final truth about himself.

He was no trapper, rancher, prospective husband or regular citizen; never had been and never could be.

He was a drifter and wanderer, a hunter and dreamer who might never stay more than six weeks in one place again for the rest of his life.

He drew rein atop the ridge as the sleet blew itself out and a brighter light filled the stormy sky.

Steel blue eyes stared ahead at his life.

Before him lay the wilderness.

We do hope that you have enjoyed reading this large print book.

Did you know that all of our titles are available for purchase?

We publish a wide range of high quality large print books including:
Romances, Mysteries, Classics
General Fiction
Non Fiction and Westerns

Special interest titles available in large print are:
The Little Oxford Dictionary
Music Book, Song Book
Hymn Book, Service Book

Also available from us courtesy of Oxford University Press:
Young Readers' Dictionary
(large print edition)
Young Readers' Thesaurus
(large print edition)

For further information or a free brochure, please contact us at:
Ulverscroft Large Print Books Ltd.,
The Green, Bradgate Road, Anstey,
Leicester, LE7 7FU, England.
Tel: (00 44) **0116 236 4325**
Fax: (00 44) **0116 234 0205**

DEAD IS FOR EVER

Amy Sadler

After rescuing Hope Bennett from the clutches of two trailbums, Sam Carver made a serious mistake. He killed one of the outlaws, and reckoned on collecting the bounty on Lew Daggett. But catching Sam off-guard, Daggett made off with the girl, leaving Sam for dead. However, he was only grazed and once he came to, he set out in search of Hope. When he eventually found her, he was forced into a dramatic showdown with his life on the line.

SMOKING STAR

B. J. Holmes

In the one-horse town of Medicine Bluff two men were dead. Sheriff Jack Starr didn't need the badge on his chest to spur him into tracking the killer. He had his own reason for seeking justice, a reason no-one knew. It drove him to take a journey into the past where he was to discover something else that was to add even greater urgency to the situation — to stop Montana's rivers running red with blood.

CABEL

Paul K. McAfee

Josh Cabel returned home from the Civil War to find his family all murdered by rioting members of Quantrill's band. The hunt for the killers led Josh to Colorado City where, after months of searching, he finally settled down to work on a ranch nearby. He saved the life of an Indian, who led him to a cache of weapons waiting for Sitting Bull's attack on the Whites. His involvement threw Cabel into grave danger. When the final confrontation came, who had the fastest — and deadlier — draw?

RIVERBOAT

Alan C. Porter

When Rufus Blake died he was found to be carrying a gold bar from a Confederate gold shipment that had disappeared twenty years before. This inspires Wes Hardiman and Ben Travis to swap horse and trail for a riverboat, the *River Queen*, on the Mississippi, in an effort to find the missing gold. Cord Duval is set on destroying the *River Queen* and he has the power and the gunmen to do it. Guns blaze as Hardiman and Travis attempt to unravel the mystery and stay alive.

McKINNEY'S LAW

Mike Stotter

McKinney didn't count on coming across a dead body in the middle of Texas. He was about to become involved in an ever-deepening mystery. The renegade Comanche warrior, Black Eagle, was on the loose, creating havoc; he didn't appear in McKinney's plans at all, not until the Comanche forced himself into his life. The US Army gave McKinney some relief to his problems, but it also added to them, and with two old friends McKinney set about bringing justice through his own law.

BLACK RIVER

Adam Wright

John Dyer has come to the insignificant little town of Black River to destroy the last living reminder of his dark past. He has come to kill. Jack Hart is determined to stop him. Only he knows the terrible truth that has driven Dyer here, and he knows that only he can beat Dyer in a gunfight. Ex-lawman Brad Harris is after Dyer too — to avenge his family. The stage is set for madness, death and vengeance.